D.S. MURPHY

Printed in the United States of America

First Printing, 2017

Urban Epics
Portland, OR
www.UrbanEpics.com

10 9 8 7 6 5 4 3 2 1

Prologue

The old woman appeared out of nowhere and limped down Templeton street with the support of a gnarled branch. Her skin was burned and her eyes bloodshot. Her matted hair writhed like a nest of snakes, and her floppy, basset hound ears disappeared into the folds of the dirty rags she was wearing. Protruding from her back were a pair of leathery bat wings.

The woman split into two with a great ripping noise that echoed through the cookie-cutter houses of the suburban subdivision. The second woman split again into a third—a smaller, older, and uglier woman with a vicious gleam in her eye. The three of them stopped in front of an ordinary looking house with blue trim, gazing into the windows.

"You can't be serious," Clotho said to her sisters, looking around disapprovingly. Lachesis waved her hands in the air and together they peered at the apparition; thousands of slender, silver threads that gleamed like stars against the dark night sky.

"Look sisters!" she said, pointing at one particular thread. It glowed with golden light, pulsating with power. "This is the one. This one is special."

"You said that about the last one," Atropos snorted. "Where is *she* now?"

"But can't you see how this one weaves and connects? This one will change everything. This one will restore balance."

Clotho sighed and shrugged her shoulders. "It's not like we have any other options. He is getting too powerful, I doubt we'll last another century."

"But we must," Atropos said. "If he finds us—"

"That's what the girl is for," Lachesis said, "in case we don't make it. A final precaution."

"We'll have to share our powers with her," Clotho said thoughtfully. "It's against the rules."

Atropos cackled, "Do you think he worries about following the rules? Anything is permitted if it brings him power."

"Then it's agreed," Lachesis said. "She was born three days ago. It's time."

Together they snuck towards the front of the house. Clotho whispered a spell and the door unlocked with a click. They shuffled inside, and then up the stairs. Past the bedroom, where the parents were soundly sleeping, and into the nursery. As one body, they peered forward to look at the infant in her crib. She was awake, and watching them with silent, wide eyes.

Clotho went first, pulling energy from the air and spinning it into a fine thread that shone in the moonlight. Lachesis took the ends and measured out a length in front of her, holding it up to her sisters for approval. They nodded, and together they chanted.

In the midst of darkness, light;
In the midst of death, life;
In the midst of chaos, order.
In the midst of order, chaos;
Thus has it ever been,
Thus is it now,
and Thus shall it always be.

The thread turned dark red as it was infused with their magic. Then Atropos took a pair of golden scissors from some secret pocket in her dirty robes. They sparkled in the dim light. Lachesis held the thread out over the crib and Atropos snipped it at both ends. Then Clotho took the scarlet thread and tied it around the infant's left wrist.

"What about the shears?" Atropos asked.

"We'll hide them somewhere," Clotho announced. Somewhere he will never look."

"How will she find them?" Lachesis asked.

"If she's really the one," Clotho said, "she'll know where they are and reclaim them when the time is right."

"And if she isn't?" Atropos asked.

"Then we are doomed."

The baby started to cry, but now it was alone in an empty room, waving her tiny wrists.

1

The end of my world began like any other day. I woke up on the thin, dirty pad on the cement shelf of my tiny room, and let my fingertips pass through the streams of light that fell through the ten-inch window. It was a little game I played with myself, a way to check the weather. To prepare myself mentally for the day ahead. If my fingers cast shadows against the wall, I knew it would be sunny. There were no shadows that day. I brushed my teeth and put on the only clean clothes I had, a *Sound of Music* T-shirt and pair of thick black stockings. We could only do laundry once a week and I was down to my last pair of underwear. My dark hair was tangled but I'd stopped combing it years ago. Nobody inside the institution cared about that stuff anymore.

It was all girls in my wing, except for the guards, and you did not want to look pretty for the guards. I've seen girls make that mistake before. Afterwards, a committee would decide that the oversexed, "crazy" teenage girls had seduced the pot-bellied, grown men with their wanton ways and alluring nubile bodies. "They were asking for it," the committee would say, and the guards would get off with a slap on the wrist, and the girls would sob at night for a few months, and then things would go back to normal.

It would be different if this were an ordinary school. Maybe even a normal psychiatric hospital. But the JDRI—Juvenile Detention Reform Institution, or as we liked to call it, "Juicy Dames Reliably Incarcerated"—was neither. This was the place parents sent their children when they couldn't stand to look at them anymore. That's how I ended up here anyway.

I took a minute to scrub the floor with a damp old rag—one of my most prized possessions—until the cracked stone floor practically gleamed. It was easier to see the spiders that way. I hated spiders. I'm sure I've swallowed hundreds of them in here. I imagined them crawling into my mouth when I was sleeping. All the ones I didn't spot coming and flatten with a shoe or a book. Maybe that's why my throat always feels so scratchy and tight. I'm filling up with dead spiders.

I wish I could tell you I lived in a dungeon, with rusty bars across an open space so the administration could watch us sleep, or crumbling stone walls with chains hanging in the corners... but the JDRI wasn't that bad. We were fed well. There was a big library of books for us to read. We went out daily to do community labor projects like picking up trash from the highways. We were encouraged to study and get a High School Equivalency Diploma before we turned eighteen and were released to our own care. They even gave us $10 of pocket money a week to spend during the weekend shopping trips.

Things didn't have to get ugly, if we followed the rules. And I always followed the rules. Which could have made me unpopular in here. Most of the other girls really were delinquents. Some of them were hard-ass bitches. But there weren't many murderers. Just me.

There were no mirrors in JDRI, but I'd stolen a metal tray for that purpose and quickly checked my reflection in its dull, scratched surface. Each month we got a pile of donated clothing, but it was mostly crap that either fit like a parachute, or was meant for toddlers. I'd learned years ago to make my own clothes. I enjoyed feeling the cold, hard metal of the needle against my skin, the repetitive motion of stitching fabric together. Even the unavoidable pricks of pain brought me a perverse pleasure. I'd watch the blood bead up from the wound before sucking it clean.

My favorite sweater was a patchwork of different shades of inky, dark squares of colorless void. I made plain gray skirts that hung to my knees, with cute or funny T-shirts sewn in ironically. My cherished all-star high-tops were black and frayed—I'd saved up for months to buy them two years ago and I only took them off to sleep. I wrapped a black scarf around my neck and pulled my slender, black leather gloves over my pale fingers. I bought them in a vintage shop last year, and wore them even in the summer time.

The only piece of color in my dark ensemble was the chunk of brightly colored lego blocks I wore around my neck. My little brother was working on it the day he died. It's unfinished, so I'll never know what it was meant to be. I wore it to remind myself of what life had been like, before my curse ruined everything.

I grabbed a pair of dark aviator glasses before leaving my room. People say the eyes are the windows to the soul, and I didn't want anybody to know I was home. Pretty eyes are an invitation for people to start talking with you. Mine are teal blue, but with a dark ring around the edges that makes them distinctive. When I was young, people would say "my, what extraordinary eyes you have!" and then pat me on the head or give me candy. But that was before my brother died. Before they found out I'd killed him.

The air outside was crisp and cool—October in the Pacific Northwest. Although it was overcast, the gray light was sharp and blinding. With my sunglasses, black clothes and tanged dark hair, I looked like a psychopath. Which is just how I wanted it.

It helped fuel the rumors that people spread about me. That I'd butchered my family. That I'd torn the heart out of my boyfriend and eaten it. Jessie, my best friend in this place, had even started a rumor that I could kill someone just by looking at them. If I pulled down my shades even a little bit, the younger girls ran away in terror—and some of the older ones, too.

Nobody knew my real story except Mrs. Taylor, JDRI's principal and warden, and Jessie. I'd told her all about it our first year here, when we were both nine. That was almost eight years ago. Even the guards usually left me alone. They didn't know the truth. That I felt guilty even for the spiders I killed. That the sight of blood made me queasy. That I was basically a huge wimp.

Unlike Jessie, who was actually a badass. She worked out in the gym facility, was just about the tallest girl in the school, and met all obstacles with a flurry of punches. She ended up here after breaking her step-father's nose. Most people thought Jessie and I were together, another notion we did nothing to correct. Better the other girls think I belong to Jessie than constantly getting hit on by all the lesbos in JDRI.

"Kaidance!" Mrs. Taylor shouted my name during breakfast announcements. I froze, a half-eaten English muffin hanging out of my mouth. "You've got a visitor. Come with me after breakfast."

The whispering began immediately. There were 247 girls in the North Wing of JDRI, and weeks could go by without a single one of them getting a visitor. We were the unwanted dregs of society.

My parents hadn't come to see me in almost three years. During that last visit, I believed they might be coming to take me home. Maybe they'd finally forgiven me. Instead, they told me they were moving, and it would be hard for them to make the trip any longer. The following year just about killed me. It wasn't that I was hurting myself, not deliberately. I just couldn't be bothered to eat, to bathe, to roll out of bed. You could set me in a corner and I'd be furniture until you moved me somewhere else. I smoked whenever I could find a cigarette, and I was so thin you could hear my bones jangle together. They'd tried drugs, counseling, punishment—nothing worked.

Jessie had saved me, by bringing me Sarah. She was nine, the same age we'd been when we got to JDRI, and had dark brown eyes and golden hair that reminded me of my brother. She had severe panic attacks and wild tantrums that were like a tempest. If something set her off, she would tear down the fucking building. Sarah had all the rage I felt inside but never allowed myself to release. Sarah was Kali, my little goddess of destruction. I became one of the few things that soothed her, and caring for her brought me out of my depression.

"A visitor, huh?" Jessie kicked me under the table. "Expecting anybody?"

I snorted, "Yeah it's probably just my fairy godmother, come to take me to the ball."

"It could be a handsome prince," Jessie smirked.

"I'd settle for five minutes with the gardener," I joked.

Sarah cracked a smile, even though she wasn't into boys yet. She was used to us talking about them. Then she raised her eyebrows at me, asking a silent question.

And that ignited a tiny part of my brain apparently still reserved for hope. I hadn't felt it in a long time, so I was kind of surprised it showed up at all. It *could* be my parents. After all, who else would it be? Nobody else even knew I existed. But I clenched my fists and squashed the thought. Hope was dangerous. Hope didn't belong in JDRI. One brief moment of hope could lead to months of disappointment.

After breakfast I was excused from chores and followed Mrs. Taylor into the guest lounge. It wasn't like those things you see in prisons, with the glass wall and people speaking through phones. This room was actually one of the nicest places in the building. We used it for parties and game nights. They wanted to show visitors how comfortable we were in here. There were plush couches and antique leather chairs, but I knew they were just for show.

We weren't allowed to sit on them unless we had a visitor. In the center of the room was a line of tables. Mrs. Taylor had me sit down at one of these and wait for my guest. I scanned the bookshelf for any new titles but was disappointed, as I had been the last three times I checked. With a sigh I grabbed a dog-eared copy of a self-help book I'd read a dozen times and flipped through it.

When the door opened and my visitor stepped inside, I took a sharp breath. He was wearing a tailored gray suit with a blood red tie. His hair was slicked back away from his light blue eyes. He saw me and flashed a dazzling smile, with teeth that were too white and straight to be real. He could have easily been one of the models Jessie and I drooled over a few weeks ago, when we found a GQ magazine in the recycling.

In his presence, the guest lounge, which I'd always thought of as classy, was revealed for what it really was: cheap furniture with a faux-antique gloss. Mostly mass-produced stuff from bargain stores. The suit this guy was wearing looked like it was worth more than everything else in this room put together.

He sat down across from me, sliding into the chair with the grace and power of an athlete, and very carefully set a polished leather briefcase on the table. I clenched my teeth together to make sure my jaw wasn't hanging open. I'd never been this close to a guy this hot before.

"Kaidance Monroe." It wasn't a question, so I nodded my head.

"Would you mind…?" he tapped at the corner of his eye.

I removed my sunglasses. Suddenly self-conscious, I reached up and smoothed out my tangled hair.

"And the gloves," he said, nodding at my hands.

"I don't take these off," I said.

"Indulge me," he said, "I've come a long way to see you."

I considered refusing, but now I was curious. *Who was this guy?* Whatever he was doing here,

I wanted to know what he had to say. I pulled off the gloves, one by one, and set them on the table. His eyes flickered to my arm, drawn to the dark red line that wrapped around my wrist like a bracelet. I pulled the sleeve of my sweater up to hide it, my cheeks heating up. It looked like a scar, and people usually thought I'd done it to myself—that I'd tried to cut my whole hand off. I'd had it as long as I can remember, but I hated having to talk about it.

He smiled at me again, and my heart fluttered. His skin was perfect and smooth. He looked way too young to be dressed like a stock broker. He reached inside his jacket pocket and pulled out a small notepad.

"You were admitted nine years ago after the death of your little brother, after a court found you guilty of his murder, is that right?"

I shifted uncomfortably in my seat. *So much for prince charming.* I hadn't talked about my brother's death for years. Why bring it up now? I realized I still had a smile on my face—an involuntary response to the one he'd given me—and I let it drop. For some reason, I didn't want this guy to think I was a psychopath.

"But you always maintained, according to court records and the psychologist's report, that you were innocent, that you were trying to save him, not push him in front of the car. Correct?"

"Not that it did me any good," I muttered. He nodded sympathetically, making a note with an expensive looking pen.

"And the reason that the court decided against you," he said, reading his notes, "was that you told your parents about the red Toyota that was going to kill your brother several months before it happened. Since they couldn't understand how you'd known the color or model of the car in advance, it was concluded that you must have planned out your brothers' death and taken action when you saw a car that would support your claims. As the psychologist put it, you were acting out for attention and desperate to make your parents believe you by "proving" your lies. You were tried as a minor—you were only nine years old after all—and they decided you'd be better off in facility where you could get the supervision and care you needed."

"My parents couldn't even look at me when they said goodbye," I said. "They just left me here." I felt emotions that had taken years to bury begin to stir in my stomach. *Not good.* What did this guy want? Why was he bringing up all this ancient history? Were they going to open an inquiry? Would they re-open the case? I let my fingers curl around my lego necklace. It had become a security blanket of sorts. Touching it reminded me that bad things could result from good intentions.

He reached down and opened the latches of his briefcase, and lifted it up slowly. I squealed when a gray kitten with crystal blue eyes crawled out. I hadn't seen a kitten since I was a little girl. I *loved* kittens. And for just a second, I let down my defenses. Before my brain knew what my hands were doing, I reached down and scooped the kitten to my chest. I rubbed my cheek against the soft fur on his back.

Then I realized, with horror, that I'd taken off my gloves. I felt the warmth of the tiny body through my pale fingers, and that's when I saw the vision. My face scrunched together, trying to block it out, but it filled my brain—until nothing else existed but the kitten and the hammer. The strong blows crushing its poor little skull. The blood. I yelped and dropped the kitten, my heart pounding. It meowed and sunk its razor sharp little claws into my arm, holding on until I could set him down on the table gently.

My visitor watched this whole exchange smugly, a smile playing on his lips. And that's when I knew, this had been a test. And I'd just failed.

2

The first time I saw death I was five years old. My mother was pregnant with Charlie, my little brother, and my parents sent me next door to play with the neighbor's daughter, Michelle, who was two years older than me. She mostly invented role-plays which featured her as queen and me as servant girl, so she could boss me around. In the afternoon, her mother walked me home and grabbed my hand to cross the street.

That's when I saw her, lying in a hospital bed, her eyes wide as she tried to wheeze another breath. Her strength left her and the blips from the machine near her body turned into one solid beeeeeeeeeeep. I remember smelling chemicals and urine. Two weeks later my mother explained to me that Michelle's mom had died and Michelle was moving away to live with her father in another state.

The next time it was a classmate in Kindergarten. I told him he was going to fall from a tree and break his head open on the sidewalk. I described the yellow shirt and blue pants he was wearing. When he wouldn't listen, I drew a picture of the scene to the best of my abilities. I used a lot of red crayon, all around his head, to show the blood. That's when the trips to the psychologist started.

I began to understand that something was wrong with me—that normal people don't see other people's deaths before they happen. So when the psychologist asked me every week whether I still saw people dying, I started saying no.

Eventually I learned, if I touched someone and saw their death, they were going to die within a few months. I didn't know exactly when. I just knew *how.* But I also learned that people got mad at me when I talked about it. So I started wrapping my hands up in my sleeves and avoiding contact with people. With this new habit, I went several years without seeing anyone die. My parents thought I'd gotten better. I was just better at hiding it.

One day I was wrestling at home with Charlie, and saw him get hit by a red car at the park near our house. I begged my parents to move to another town. I screamed for days. The visits to the psychologist resumed. My parents fought at night about what was wrong with me, and how to fix it. But this time I couldn't pretend that I hadn't seen anything. This was my little brother. I was fighting to save his life. I just had to make everybody understand. So I investigated. I grabbed his arm, trying to hold onto the vision, trying to slow it down and absorb every detail. I drew pictures of the car. I knew it was a Toyota Corolla—I skipped school one day to visit a car lot and check—but I couldn't see the license plate, no matter how many times I looked.

They put me on medication that made me feel slow. They said I had a morbid fascination with death, and was acting out for attention. That's when I realized it was up to me. I was the only one who could save him. So I followed him around everywhere. I walked him to every class. I never let him out of my sight. I threw a tantrum every time we went to the park, but they dragged me there anyway—it was the only one near the house, and they thought it would be good for me. To prove to me that nothing bad would happen.

I tried to keep Charlie in the exact middle of the park, playing some game that kept us seated the whole time. But one day, a pair of older boys were kicking a soccer ball, and it rolled past us, and Charlie jumped up and chased after it. I raced after him. I felt like I was in a game of Duck Duck Goose—trying to catch him before he made it around the circle. My arms outstretched, I missed him by inches as he stepped out into the street and was hit by the car I'd seen months before. I watched, horrified, as his little body flew fifteen feet forward and slammed into the concrete with a sickening crunch. Then I sunk onto the curb and started sobbing.

I felt the guilt in an abstract sense. He was dead because I saw that red Toyota Corolla coming—two and a half months before it actually hit him. Even with all that time I'd failed to stop it from happening. *I killed him.* Not literally, but I still felt like it was somehow my fault.

My parents had a different take on things. Since I was obviously bat shit crazy, and had been talking about how Charlie was going to get hit by a red car for months, and since eye witnesses had seen me run towards him at full speed with my arms out in front of me, they all assumed I'd pushed him.

Everybody believed that I killed my little brother, just to prove I could see the future. That I was a twisted, sick, monster of a child who couldn't be allowed to go to public school anymore. My mother couldn't handle the looks people gave her, or how they pulled their children away from me when they saw us coming. My father started locking their bedroom door at night. They were afraid of me. Afraid of what else I might do.

That's how I ended up here. It's probably where I belong. After dozens of appointments with JDRI's resident psychiatrist, Pam Miller, I wasn't even sure I hadn't pushed my brother. Was I mis-remembering what happened? I had to be—as everyone kept telling me, seeing the future was impossible. And even if I *had* really seen Charlie's death, that probably meant I'd somehow caused it, so I was guilty either way. In the last few years, I started having more questions. In witnessing someone's death, did I seal their fate? Would it inevitably happen afterwards, or could it still be changed? But it wasn't exactly something that could be tested. If I knew about someone's death, and said nothing, didn't that make me responsible? The best practice was to keep my hands covered and my head down. I don't let people touch me anymore. Not my fingertips, not my skin, not my heart.

Normally I'd be on one of several work shifts in the morning and then choose between a number of activities or self-study classes in the afternoon. But since I was temporarily excused from normalcy, I snuck outside into the small courtyard and sat down against the single tree on the property, a sprawling oak. Just past the perimeter fence was forest of cedars, with long pine needles that turned brown and fell like snow in the autumn. The fence was more decorative than functional—if we really wanted to slip out or run away, it wasn't that hard. But the few who had tried, begged to be let back in. JDRI wasn't that bad of a place to be, all things considered. A teenage girl with no address and no income can only do so many things on the streets to survive, and none of them ended happily.

I brought a book with me, but I kept reading the same lines over and over. I couldn't get the mysterious visitor out of my mind. Did he bring that kitten just to test my reaction? Did that mean he believed me—or was he just confirming how crazy I was? Maybe my parents had been thinking of letting me come home, and had sent him to check whether I was ready. *And I'd blown it.*

I didn't hear the footsteps approach until a shadow fell across my lap. I looked up to see a man in a guard uniform with an underachieving, scraggly beard. I hadn't seen him before.

"Hey sexy," he smiled with a grin that made my blood run cold.

I looked around and was suddenly aware of how quiet it was. I could hear the limbs creaking in the wind above me, and the caw of a crow flying overhead. I wondered if any of the other staff could see us. But a guard wouldn't use inappropriate language like that if anybody else was around. He knew we were alone.

"I heard you liked books," he said, squatting down beside me. "I thought maybe we could make a trade," he whispered, leaning in closer. "You know, you rub my back, I rub yours?"

He smiled lewdly. Apparently, he'd taken this job to hit on girls who couldn't run away. And unfortunately, it could have worked... on another girl. We don't have much interaction with the opposite sex here, and many girls might have been willing to rub his "back" in exchange for an expensive gift or favor. I wasn't one of them.

"You don't look like you know your way around a good book," I said. "Or a woman, for that matter," I added quietly.

"You'll change your tune, once you get to know me," he said.

Where do they find these guys?

"Now be a good girl and—"

"Didn't they tell you?" Jessie said, walking up behind us. "Kaidance is one of the worst offenders in here."

I smiled at her in relief. The guard glanced at her, then looked back at me skeptically. My thin arms and wrists made me look frail. An easy target for abuse.

"A literal man-eater, if you know what I mean, *Dennis*," she continued, reading his name off his name tag. "She cut off her boyfriend's junk and fried it up like a sausage. That's how she ended up here. I'd watch out if I were you."

Dennis's eyes widened and he leaned away from me a bit. I smiled at him—the mad dog smile with the twitching right eye it had taken me months to perfect. And then very carefully, I licked my lips, in a way I hoped was both sexy and terrifying. He stood up and leered at the both of us, his fingers tracing the handle of the Taser on his utility belt.

"Whatever," he said finally. "Just trying to be friendly."

"Try somewhere else," Jessie said, holding up her middle finger.

"You haven't had to save me from creeps for a long time," I said, as we watched Dennis disappear into the main building.

"Yeah, a month or two at least. Either they've dropped their hiring standards, or you're just getting too cute for your own good," Jessie teased.

I rolled my eyes.

"So, it's Saturday." She brushed the ground next to me before sitting down.

"Again?" I asked.

"Yup, don't be surprised. Comes every week."

"Don't give me that—I mean, another party, right?"

"Well, I got a note from Ryan, that guy we met a couple of weeks back. He sent me a *letter* asking me to a party. How sweet is that?"

We weren't allowed phones in JDRI. People could call us, but they might monitor the calls. And they'd open any packages. But they don't read our mail. We're teenage girls, not terrorists.

The staff probably already knew about the hole in the fence surrounding the main buildings, the one we used to sneak out at night. They just didn't care enough to fix it.

"He's going to pick you up?"

"*Us* up." She corrected. "But no, he isn't—it's a cemetery party."

I wrinkled my nose.

Past the hole in the fence, through the cedar forest, was a road. Sometimes girls would hitchhike to town in the back of a pickup truck, or have a guy pick them up in exchange for a hand job. On the other side of the road was a cemetery.

"A party in a cemetery seems crazy. Even for us."

"No, it's cool," Jessie said. "It's a Halloween party. It's perfect."

"Go without me," I said, crossing my arms.

"Absolutely not. You're going and there's nothing you can say or do to stop it. You'll be eighteen soon. You've got to learn how to survive in the real world. Think of it as practice."

She had a point. Once released, I'd be expected to take care of myself. I was already dreading the thought of job interviews. I was painfully bad at small talk.

"We don't have costumes," I said.

"It's casual," Jessie said, with a triumphant grin. She knew she'd won. "Besides, I made you something in arts and crafts." She pulled a dark bundle out of her bag and held it up to her face. It was a mask, made of sleek black feathers and paper mache. The curved beak hung down over her nose.

"How many birds did you have to kill to make that?" I asked.

"Just one," she said. "But I didn't kill it. We found a dead raven near the fence, and they let me use it. Turns out I can look forward to a promising career in taxidermy."

"So you want me to wear a dead bird on my face so you can go hang out with a cute boy?" I asked. Jessie smiled her most beguiling smile, and batted her eyelids in pretend pleading.

"When do we leave?" I sighed.

3

After my brother died, I spent a lot of time at his grave. The cemetery was a few miles outside of town, and I rode my bicycle there every chance I got. That was before they pulled me out of school, and before I got sent to JDRI. I picked flowers to put on the grave, and sometimes split my lunch with him. What I'm trying to say is, cemeteries remind me of my dead brother. And I don't need reminding.

"I'm going home," I said, crossing my arms as we approached the black iron gate, and the granite headstones and marble statues behind it.

"Stay an hour, then we'll discuss it," Jessie said, grabbing my hand and pulling me forward. "It's Halloween after all. And you look great." Jessie had rubbed charcoal all around my eyes, which made my eyes even more startling.

Sarah tied my dark hair into a bird's nest of a bun, with tangles and spikes and long feathers jutting out to the sides. Then she pinned the mask so it rested on my forehead. She'd begged us to let her come, but she was only eleven. Way too young for a party. Plus, if we got caught sneaking out, the punishment would be way worse if Sarah was with us.

I'd put on a pair of jeans and the same patchwork sweater I'd been wearing all day. As we entered the cemetery, I wished I had an amazing black dress like I'd seen in fashion magazines, with sequins that glittered in the moonlight. I imagined the long tails floating silently behind me, hovering just above the cold dirt, as I drifted, like death, among the gravestones.

The party was a mix of kids from JDRI and some local kids who weren't afraid to mix it up with us nutters. Most people were wearing cheap plastic masks or funny clothes, but nobody was seriously dressed up. Then later, more people arrived, until it was mostly townies. I realized suddenly that this was the first *real* teenage party I'd ever been to, where the majority of attendees were just regular kids. It was a good chance to meet people who didn't act like they were waiting for you to pull out a knife and stab them.

JDRI was co-ed, but the boys were in a separate wing. We had occasional mixers and social events, and even some shared classes or rooms, but the pickings were slim. There were a couple decent looking guys, but of course they all had baggage, and they'd hook up with whichever girl made it easy for them. I wasn't in the habit of throwing myself at guys, and with my reputation, few boys dared to even talk to me. Not that I was obsessed with boys or anything. But it's not like there was much else to think about.

Somebody brought boxed wine and plastic cups, and cranked up the radio. Jessie found Ryan, and introduced me to Ryan's friend Paul. Then she and Ryan said they were going to get another drink and disappeared. I knew I was being set up when Paul started asking me boring questions about JDRI. At first I tried to be civil, but he quickly got on my nerves. I was at a party, why couldn't I pretend to be normal? At least he didn't ask me why my parents abandoned me, or why I'd killed my brother. Paul made a good effort, but eventually my scowl and monosyllable answers wore away his confidence. He mumbled something about finding his friend and left me standing by myself. I refilled my plastic cup and sipped it from the shadows.

Dozens of candles in big glass jars were scattered around the area—on top of headstones and nestled between tree branches. They cast little orbs of light that were both charming and ominous. They'd even used the candles to make a big skull and bones symbol on the ground. Ryan and Jessie came back and I was just starting to have fun when I felt someone staring at me.

I turned and saw a guy just outside the ring of kids, leaning against a tall, narrow tombstone with a cross on top. His hair was so blond it looked white in the darkness, and his eyes were an unusual golden amber that flickered in the candlelight. I broke eye contact and tried to ignore him, but when I glanced back he was still looking at me. No, more than that. He was *glaring* at me. I could feel his gaze against my skin, scraping like sandpaper. It gave me goosebumps. I waited for him to smile or wave or something, but his face was expressionless. He was just sitting there, *watching* me, like a creepy statue.

Finally I couldn't take it anymore.

"I'm going to head back," I said to Jessie.

"Already?" she said, frowning. She'd been flirting with Ryan, and now they were holding hands. It made me feel lonely, which made me feel stupid. She'd dragged me here, but I didn't want to ruin her night.

"It's cool, I'll walk back myself. You should stay."

"You sure?" she asked, looking at me and then back at Ryan.

"It's a short walk. I'll be fine."

Ryan whispered something in her ear, and she laughed.

"Okay, be safe," Jessie said.

"You too," I answered, giving her a pointed look. "Knock when you get in. Be back before midnight or I'll eat Ryan's liver." He gulped as I made slurping noises.

I turned around to hide my smile, then walked across the street and into the woods. I hadn't gone far when a shadow startled me. I looked up to see a figure blocking my path. It was that weird blond kid again. *How had he gotten in front of me?* I thought about rejoining the party, but that would be silly. And I wasn't far, I could still hear music and voices. I could scream if I had to. I crossed my arms and soldiered forward.

"Can I help you?" I asked coldly as I stomped towards him. He looked surprised for a moment, as if he thought he'd been hiding, instead of standing in the middle of the path. His leather pants were black, but his white T-shirt stood out like a beacon in the dark forest around us. Up close, he was tall. In the moonlight his skin was almost as white and pale as his hair, and I could see the black lines of a tattoo wrapping around both of his forearms. I wondered if it connected in the middle of his back, then pictured him naked, which made blood rush through my body.

"Sorry," he murmured. "I was just... watching."

"Yeah I saw that. Stalk much?"

Somehow I could still see the honey color of his eyes. They shone like a predator's in the darkness. I shivered, and my skin tingled.

"I'm just looking for somebody. A friend. I thought they might be here." *In the middle of the woods? Not likely.*

"Got stood up, huh? Don't sweat it. Anyway, I'm headed back to... back home," I said, stepping around him. I didn't feel like explaining I was going to sneak back *into* a juvenile detention center.

"I'll walk you," he said, falling in step with me.

"Please don't," I said. "I mean, it's fine. I can manage myself."

"It's dark. I can't let you walk through the woods alone."

"Who says chivalry is dead?" I said, rolling my eyes. This guy was tough to get rid of.

"I'm no gentleman," he said, with a sad half-smile. "But I'd feel better escorting you. There are more dangers around than you realize."

"How do I know you're not dangerous?" I said. I was teasing, kind of, but he seemed to consider the question seriously. He looked up at the sky for a few seconds as if he could divine the answer, then nodded to himself. "We're already alone in the woods. I *could* be dangerous. But since I haven't hurt you yet, I probably don't mean you any harm. At least not tonight." I looked over for the smirk I was sure would be there, but his face was stiffer than the dead raven on my head.

"That was way too honest of an answer," I muttered. We walked in silence for a few moments. "Well it's really uncomfortable letting a total stranger walk me home, so can I have your name at least?"

"Puriel," he said.

Weird name.

"I'm Kaidance. Kai. What school do you go to?"

"I'm not a student," he said. He didn't look much older than me.

"Work around here?" I asked.

"My duties take me many places," he said. "I'm here for a particular project."

"In Chehalis? Lucky you," I snorted. "Have you seen the 1916 steam engine yet? Or the Vintage Motorcycle Museum? Those are pretty much the only things here."

"It's not without its charms," he said with the hint of a smile. It was the first sign that he might not be a serial killer. I glanced at the intricate tattoos climbing up his muscular arms. He was weird, no question. But oddly fascinating.

The loud crack of a broken branch ripped through the woods. Before I could react, Puriel shoved me backwards and flung himself in front of me. He moved so quickly I stumbled off the path in surprise. I cried out when a sharp branch dug into my cheek.

"What the *hell!*" I glared at him, "What do you think is out there, bears? It's probably a possum or a raccoon. There's nothing at all dangerous around here."

He kept his hands out, blocking my path. His narrowed eyes searched the woods around us. Finally, he grunted and turned back to look at me.

"Sorry," he said. He reached his hand up to my chin and tilted my head to see where the branch had scratched me. "You're bleeding," he said. Before I could stop him, he licked his thumb and then brushed it against my cheek to wipe away the blood. It felt wet and warm, almost like a kiss.

That's when I saw the stars. I thought I must have blacked out. My vision was filled with millions of them, whole galaxies, everything converging together into one blinding light, and then nothingness. Just empty, black void. It all happened in less than a second, and I instinctively swatted his hand away from my face.

My sight returned and I was looking into Puriel's golden eyes. We were so close I could see small flecks of yellow in them. He was peering at me with curiosity, like he was trying to see inside me. I wished I had my sunglasses on. Then I realized I was tilted backwards, and Puriel had one arm supporting me from behind. My body was inches away from his, and I could smell vanilla candles, decomposing earth, and cedar—wrapped in the warmth of his skin.

"Don't ever touch me again," I said, putting my palms on his chest and pushing him firmly away from me. As I stumbled backwards, I heard Jessie calling my name and spun towards her.

"There you are!" she said, "Man you walk slow. Party's a bust. I thought I heard your voice. Talking to yourself again?"

I glanced behind me, then turned and looked in all directions. I was completely alone. It was just me, the moonlight, and acres of tall, dark fir trees. For the first time in my life, I thought I might really be going crazy.

4

The next morning I stood in front of the makeshift mirror in my room with my palm against my cheek. There was no mark at all from the night before. Not even a scratch—though I was certain that branch had drawn blood. On the way home I asked Jessie if she'd seen a guy with white blond hair and warm yellow eyes at the party. She hadn't. I wondered if anybody else had seen him. I remember the feeling of his thumb on my cheek. If Puriel wasn't real, I didn't know how much I could trust my senses.

I terrified myself with the thought that Jessie was just an imaginary friend I made up and had been talking to for the past eight years. Maybe that's why everyone stayed away from me. I was so relieved in the morning when I saw her talking to other girls, my eyes filled with tears. The party had been real. I still had mud stains on my clothes, not to mention a slight headache from the wine. But walking home with Puriel seemed just as real. Had he really even been there? If so how had he disappeared so quickly?

And why didn't I have a mark on my cheek where the branch scratched me? And what had been that weird vision I saw when he touched me—I'd never seen anything like that before. It was like the Big Bang in reverse. I'd always assumed I was tough enough to survive in JDRI. I'd do my time, then get out and start a normal life. Now I wasn't so sure.

To get out, I had to pass a final psych test. If I wasn't deemed sane, I wouldn't be released. I'd go to a *real* mental institution; the kind that you can't escape from. And I could be there forever. The thought of being locked up for the rest of my life petrified me. I was so wrapped up in my fears, I almost didn't notice that Sarah was acting weird. It wasn't until lunch that I saw it, in the reflection of the shine of Dennis's bald patch as he walked by our table, strutting like a peacock fanning its feathers. A flicker of fear on Sarah's face.

It was a fleeting moment. Nobody else could have seen it. *But I did.* I looked at Dennis and then back at her. Sarah had been hanging out with us for the past few years. Even though she was so young, people didn't mess with her. She had nothing to be afraid of, until Dennis showed up. And in that second, that second when I realized Dennis must have done something to Sarah, something that scared her, I was ready to rip out his intestines and hang him out my window. In my mind I watched him kick and struggle against his own innards, his blood dripping around him like rain, gasping for his last breath.

He saw me staring and sauntered over.

"Hey there, darling," he said. "Change your mind about that book?"

I reached over and took Sarah's hand.

"Did he hurt you?" I whispered, leaning towards her. "Did he *touch* you?"

Her face told me everything I needed to know.

"Listen, Dennis," Jessie said. "You're new so you don't know how things work yet. We'll forgive you this time. But you need to get the fuck out of here."

"Is that how it's going to be?" Dennis said. He undid the clasp on his belt and pulled out his Taser, holding it in front of him like a pistol. "I'm really going to enjoy this," he said, in a buttery voice that made my skin crawl. "Now be a good girl and finish your fucking potatoes."

When I was little, I'd learned to be silent. The more I talked, the less people liked me. I'd been a good girl, even after my parents left me at JDRI. I never made a fuss. I studied hard. But good behavior didn't bring my parents back. *Be a good girl?*

That's what people have been telling me my whole life. And I always was. I cleaned my plate. I kept my room tidy. I never complained. Where had it gotten me? Abandoned by my parents. Forgotten by the whole world. And now my best friend was about to be electrocuted by some asshole guard, who thought he could do whatever he wanted to us in here. And he was probably right.

That's what I was thinking just before I slammed my lunch tray across Dennis' face. I watched him stumble backwards, a drop of blood sliding down his forehead, then sat down and continued eating.

5

Remember when I said that JDRI wasn't like a dungeon? I was wrong. I'd never been in solitary before. The cellars were over a hundred years old, with thick wooden beams in the ceilings. They'd been divided into "discipline rooms." When we became too much of a disturbance, or a danger to ourselves and others, they'd lock us up until we calmed down. Nobody could hear us scream or cry or bang on the walls down here. The room was half the size of my regular bedroom, with jagged cracks running down the stone walls. Spiderwebs clung to the corners. And for the first time since I got to JDRI, my door was locked from the outside.

All I could think about was getting back to Sarah and Jessie. I hated not knowing what was going on. I was so frustrated and angry I wanted to scream. But I'd already indulged myself with one violent outbreak today. I needed to pull myself together, or at least act like I had, so they'd let me get back to my friends. Dinner consisted of French fries and a corndog. They'd pulled out the little wooden stick so I had to eat with my fingers. They didn't want to give me any weapons. After eating I leaned against the cracked wall, trying to make myself comfortable on the rusty bedsprings. They creaked loudly whenever I moved.

I noticed the smell first. Not the ordinary smell of rat poop and moldy wood. It was a smell of roses and wildflowers, but sweeter, like honey. It filled the room like a cloud. Then I heard the voice. *Puriel's* voice.

"Do you ever feel guilty?"

It sounded like he was sitting right next to me. I jumped up and searched the tiny room, but I was alone. I looked through the glass window in the door, but I couldn't see anyone outside. Great. I'm smelling things and hearing voices. Aren't those signs of a brain tumor?

"About the things you do?" the voice said again. I put my ear against the wall. Maybe he was in the cell next to mine?

"How did you get in here?" I asked.

"I didn't believe it at first, you know. About your brother. But after the way you attacked that guard, I can see what you're really capable of. I just want to know, whether you ever feel guilty about the things you do. The people you hurt."

I felt my blood run cold. Who was this guy, and how did he know about my brother? Or was this really just in my head?

"What are you, my conscience?" I asked.

"Don't you believe in Judgment? Sin?"

Oh shit. I knew what was going on now. He was one of those handsome youth pastors who dressed cool to convert teens to Jesus. He wasn't stalking me, he was trying to save me.

I groaned. "Please, just go away. Did Mrs. Taylor send you here to console me? Teach me how to be a better person?"

"I wasn't sent to talk to you. Actually I wasn't supposed to talk to you at all," he said. "But I'm curious. I'm just trying to figure you out."

"I'm not a puzzle," I snapped.

"You have the power to destroy, but you aren't responsible enough to use it. Now I know why he sent me. You're dangerous."

"You're not real," I said, willing it to be true. Nobody had seen Puriel but me. Even though JDRI wasn't exactly Fort Knox, there's no way some total stranger would sneak in to talk to me about my sins. And he couldn't know about Charlie. I was losing my mind, and now I was talking to myself. I needed to get my shit together. I pulled my pillows over my head and rocked myself to sleep, willing the voices to stop. And they did.

When I opened my eyes again I was in a meadow. The light was dim, and seemed to come up from the ground. The meadow stretched out on all sides over the horizon. I should call it something else, not a meadow, but I had the sense that somewhere it ended. It was finite, limited. Not boundless. Somewhere beyond the reaches of my vision this smooth, grassy plain of wild flowers ended in rocky mountains, or an impenetrable forest. It was contained. But then the landscape shifted. It was the same meadow, but now it was up on top of a hill, and I could look across narrow valleys and see other hills, some gentle and sloping, some rugged and steep. The grass was sage green, with isolated patches of red wildflowers that pushed up in sporadic patterns. I could smell rosemary and lavender. It was the most beautiful place I'd ever seen. Enchanted somehow. Mystical.

At the top of the hill was a giant tree, its branches reaching up into the sky. When I walked closer to it, I found a deer and a goat nibbling on its leaves. The startled deer ran when I approached, but the goat just kept eating. Some kind of rot infected the trunk, and when I touched it, pieces of bark crumbled and fell, leaving sticky white patches underneath. The residue clung to my fingertips, tingling.

I heard a sound behind me and turned to see an old woman coming up the hill, with buckets on the ends of a stick balanced over her shoulders. She set the buckets down and stretched, cracking her back. The first bucket was filled with pure, shining water. It looked radiant somehow, like it was glowing. She poured it onto the ground around the roots of the tree. Then she reached into the second bucket and pulled out a thick, white clay. She covered it onto the trunk of the tree like she was drywalling a house. Then she started back down the hill.

I followed her, noticing bits of ruin along the path. Shards from forgotten kingdoms. A toppled pillar that had shattered into pieces. The arm of a statue, pointing at nothing. Down the hill and around a sharp corner was the entrance to a large tunnel, surrounded by Greek characters. The woman entered and disappeared into the darkness. It looked like she'd been swallowed by a massive underground beast. The wind teased my dark hair as I hesitated, waiting to see if she would come back out.

Instead another woman emerged, older than the first. She was stooped over, and her gnarled old skin looked worse than the tree. I waited for her to pass me like the first woman had. Instead, when she was right in front of me, she looked directly into my eyes and smiled.

"It's time," she said softly. Her words resounded across the meadow, and the ground began to shake violently. Both buckets crashed to the ground, and I felt the icy water splash across my face.

6

I woke up in a cold sweat. My face was flushed and feverish, and my brain was still muddled with images from the dream. I heard heavy breathing behind me. Adrenaline coursed through my body when I realized it wasn't mine.

"Finally, some alone time," a smooth voice said. Dennis was standing in the doorway, his silhouette lit by the flickering bulb behind him that was swaying on its cord. I could just make out the white bandage on his forehead, but the rest of his face was in shadow.

"So I thought we'd skip the reading lesson and go straight for the extra credit," he said, taking a step forward. "Sound good to you, Sweetheart?"

I took a deep breath and tried not to panic. Jessie had taught me a little about fighting. Kick them in the balls or kneecaps. Punch them in the throat, or gauge out their eyeballs. I wished they didn't make us trim our fingernails so short. I could have slashed them across his face like a panther's claws. Just as I was getting ready to pounce, his eyes bulged and he made a gurgling noise. His fingertips clutched together like he was trying to catch a passing moth. For a second, I thought I'd somehow killed him with my mind, but when he slumped over I saw the knife sticking out of his neck. The man standing behind him had short dark hair and bright blue eyes. *Briefcase man.*

"Thanks for opening the door, mate," he said, kicking the corpse out of the way. He stepped over the body that used to be Dennis, and then reached down to grab the knife. It came out with a sickening sound and a spurt of blood. I felt like I was going to puke. Briefcase man wiped the knife off on Dennis' shirt, then wrapped it in a handkerchief and tucked it into a pocket inside his leather jacket. He was wearing dark jeans and a T-shirt—much more casual than what he'd been wearing last time I saw him, but it suited him more.

"Shall we go?" he said, fixing his light blue eyes on me and holding out a hand to help me up.

My arms were trembling. I crossed them and stuck my hands in my armpits. I was 90% sure this was another dream. The other 10% came from the slightly metallic, sickly-sweet scent in the air that made the hairs on my arms stand up. I felt like a prickly cactus—all sharp edges and afraid to touch anything.

"I'm pretty sure this is off limits to visitors," I said weakly.

"This isn't a visit," he said, "It's an intervention."

"You *killed* him," I said.

"Are you complaining?" he asked.

"What are you doing here?"

"I'm here for you. You don't belong in here. You don't deserve to be treated like this. You're special. And you're important."

“Important to who?” I asked, my mind racing to catch up. I was like, 60% sure I was still dreaming at this point. From the smell, I was pretty sure dead Dennis had pissed and shit himself, which I hear is common for the recently deceased.

“Well, not your parents, obviously, and not the government that keeps you locked up in here for something you didn’t do.”

That had my attention. In all the years I’d been in here, nobody had ever believed I didn’t kill my brother, apart from Sarah and Jessie.

I felt the cold stone floor beneath me, and suddenly the room started spinning. I lurched to the side and threw up in the corner of the room. As my vomit splashed against the cold gray stones of the floor and peppered my bare ankles with bits and pieces of my last meal, I knew, for certain, deep in my gut, that this was really happening.

“Who are you?” I said, a hitch in my breath.

“A friend,” he said. “You can call me Sitri.”

“Dennis wanted to be my *friend*,” I said.

“I’m not saying I wouldn’t sleep with you,” Sitri said, raising an eyebrow. “But I’ll never lay a finger on you unless you ask me to. Now can we go please? We don’t have much time.”

“I’m not going anywhere with you,” I said, backing away from him and stepping into my own vomit. “I have friends here. I can’t leave them. Besides, I have no place to go. JDRI is my home.”

“Not anymore. I’m taking you somewhere safe. Where people like us are protected.”

“People like us—?”

“Neither the time nor the place,” he said. “I asked nicely to be polite, but I’m not leaving without you. So here are your options. Soon someone is going to find Dennis here. We’re in a locked section of the building. You’re the only one who is supposed to be here, and you attacked this man earlier today. They won’t even look for another suspect. You might get a sympathetic jury and avoid the death penalty, but with your history, they’d keep you locked up in a room like this for the rest of your life.”

He paused to let that sink in.

"Option two, you come with me right now and find out who you really are, and what you're truly capable of."

I wanted to tell him to fuck off. I wanted to say I'd rather be locked up than run away with a murderer. But he'd basically named my worst fear. If I spent any more time locked up like this, I would lose my mind—if I hadn't already. Plus, he seemed to believe me about my brother.

"I can't abandon Sarah," I said.

"They can't come with us. Not where we're going. But they'll be fine here. Jessie will take care of her."

"I have to say goodbye," I said.

Sitri grabbed my shoulders.

"Listen, after you're safe, when things have calmed down, you can come back for them if you want to. But right now, we have to leave."

I nodded, and followed him out of the room. I was dizzy, and stumbled into the wall. Sitri grabbed my hand and led me upstairs and out the front door. I was grateful I still had my gloves on—I usually take them off to sleep but hadn't bothered after they'd locked me up downstairs.

I clutched the chunk of legos around my neck, just to make sure I had it. Apart from that, there wasn't anything at JDRI I'd miss. We hurried through the main entrance and down the stairs. A red sports car was waiting for us.

"Not exactly inconspicuous," I said.

"We're not hiding," he said, opening the door for me. "We're running. And it's fast." He reached across me to fasten my seatbelt, then gunned the engine and peeled out of the parking lot.

"Can't we slow down?" I asked, after he ran through the third stoplight. "They probably won't find his body until the morning."

"Haven't you ever seen a car chase?" he asked, shifting gears. "You don't slow down."

"Who's chasing us?" I gripped the edge of my seat with my gloved fingers. I still felt nauseous and the speeding wasn't helping.

Sitri nodded to his rearview mirror. I turned around in my seat and saw a single headlight behind us. It was getting closer. Soon I could make out a pale face, with ash blond hair flying in the wind. *Puriel.*

"Wait, you can see him?" I asked.

"Um, yeah. He's right there. I hope all those years locked up didn't actually drive you mad," he said.

"They might have." I took a deep breath, so relieved I almost smiled. Whatever was going on, it was real, and I wasn't alone.

"Why is he chasing us?" I asked.

"He's not. He's chasing *you*. But don't worry," he said, pulling out a revolver the size of a small cannon. "We'll get him first." With one hand on the wheel, Sitri fired two shots behind us, shattering the back windshield. Then he fired two more. The sound of the gun made my ears ring, and the smell of burnt gunpowder filled the car.

I saw Puriel swerve on his bike, and he fell behind. When he caught up to us again, my eyes widened in disbelief. He was steering the motorcycle with his knees this time, and had both hands on a massive sword. A sword that was glowing like a blue lightsaber. *What the fuck is happening?*

When he got close enough, he swung at the car. I saw sparks and heard screeching metal as the sword carved through the car door. Another foot and it would have cut me in half. Sitri spun the wheel sharply just in time, and I saw the motorcycle swerve to avoid us. We pulled off the highway and up a dirt road. The wheels kicked up pebbles and dust behind us. Up ahead, across a field of wheat, and surrounded by a grove of giant oak trees, I saw the frame of a large house—a mansion.

When I looked back again, I saw that the motorcycle had stopped at the entrance of the dirt road. I could almost feel Puriel watching us.

"Why'd he stop?" I asked.

"Because," Sitri said, "We're home."

"I'm sorry I have to do this," Sitri said, just before he turned on a blast of icy cold water and sprayed me down. "But you stink. Plus you don't want to meet the others looking like that."

"What others?" I asked, my teeth chattering. He dried me off with a towel, rubbing my shoulders to warm me up.

"Put this on," he said, handing me a sweat suit. He turned his back and gave me some space to strip off my soiled clothes. I tossed them in a pile. The sweat suit was warm and dry. We'd driven into an underground garage filled with dozens of vehicles. Now that I had some clean clothes on, we took an elevator up to the main floor, entering into a large greeting area by the main door. The ceiling was high, and a variety of antiques fought for attention among the ornately carved furniture. The polished surfaces shone in the light of a single chandelier. A set of twin staircases ran up both sides of the room, and a hallway ran beneath them, lined with life-sized marble statues.

So this is how the other half lives.

"Is this all yours?" I asked.

"The master of the house is Able. He might still be awake, I know he was anxious to greet you himself. He'll be able to answer all your questions. But first, you must be hungry." Sitri pushed through a swinging door and we came into a large kitchen, which was a mix of traditional architecture and modern appliances. There was an island counter in the center of the room, with shelves on either side. A round wooden table against the wall was covered with cold-cuts, nuts and fruit.

"Tea?" Sitri asked. I nodded and he put on a kettle. "Help yourself," he said, nodding towards the table.

It was nothing fancy—meat, bread, butter, honey—but everything was so fresh and full of flavor. Maybe it was the shock of the night's adventure, but it was the most delicious food I remember eating. Sitri joined me at the table and we ate in silence. I knew it was wrong, to be eating so casually with a guy I'd *just seen* commit murder. But every time I tried to think clearly about what I'd experienced, my brain shut down.

After we finished eating, Sitri led me down another long hallway. Most of the house was dark, but I could see a light under a grand door at the end.

"Come in," said a deep voice just as Sitri was about to knock.

It looked like a library, the kind bookworms dreamed about, with hundreds of books on shelves that went up to the ceiling and could only be reached by a sliding ladder. In the middle of the room was a wide mahogany desk lit by two glowing desk lamps. The chair behind it was empty. It took me a second to find the man, sitting in a corner next to a small fireplace that had burned down to red embers.

"Kaidance," he said, standing up. "Welcome. I'm so glad you both made it back safely. I heard there was some trouble on the road."

All at once, the floodgates of my memory opened, churning up images that seemed more and more impossible. Dennis with a knife in his neck. Puriel with a flaming sword. Questions started pouring out of me.

"Where am I? Who are you and what do you want from me? Who was that guy chasing us? Why—"

The man held up one hand with an authority that shut me up. I looked him over in the dim light. He had dark hair, streaked with gray, and a well-trimmed beard. His eyes were so dark I could barely see his pupils. The gold cufflinks of his black suit sparkled when he moved. When he stood up he towered over me. Something about this man told me he was powerful; I could almost sense his muscles shifting, as if he were restraining himself.

"My name is Able," he said, "and this is my house. The man chasing you, I imagine, was trying to kill you."

"But why? I'm nobody."

"We'll talk about that tomorrow." He wrinkled up his nose slightly, and I could tell I still smelled like vomit. He looked at Sitri disapprovingly. "For now, take a long, warm bath, and go to bed." He nodded at Sitri and turned his back. This audience was over. I blinked my eyes slowly. I wasn't finished with him yet, but I was exhausted. My legs trembled as Sitri led me back to the hallway. We took a different staircase up to the second floor. The house was built around a central courtyard, with large windows on the inner walls looking out, and heavy gold-framed portraits on the outer walls.

The house was eerie and silent at night, and the open space hung around me like a shroud. I was relieved when Sitri opened one of the doors and gestured inside. The room was small and cozy, but as richly decorated as the rest of the house. It had a princess sized canopy bed, with four curling pillars, a reading chair with a small table near the window, and an antique desk—the kind that folds out and opens. On the other side of the room was a vanity set, with a bench and a mirror. I imagined this is what a nice European five-star hotel would look like. Or a castle. *What was I doing here?*

Sitri showed me a side door, which led to a bathroom. The large bathtub had lion's feet for legs. A mirror went across most of the wall between the cabinets. "I have my own bathroom?" I asked.

"Almost." Sitri walked across the bathroom and opened another door on the other side. I caught a glimpse of purple and black satin sheets before he shut the door again. "My room. Right next door, in case you need any help."

Help with what, taking a bath? I pictured Sitri gently stroking my shoulders with a foamy sponge, and then kissing my neck as I moaned in ecstasy. I shook my head to clear the image. I was seriously losing it.

"Help, like you helped Dennis?" I shot back at him. "No thanks." I slammed the door and pressed my back against it. I couldn't let myself forget that Sitri killed someone and kidnapped me. No matter how opulent and comfortable my new surroundings. I heard him sigh, then turn on the bath water.

"If you knew what he was thinking—what he planned to do to you..." I had a pretty good idea.

"Plus, this way you know that Sarah is safe. You don't have to worry about her." He was right about that. If I knew Dennis was still alive, I'd be frantic to get back to JDRI to protect Sarah and Jessie.

When I poked my head into the bathroom a few minutes later, Sitri was gone and steam covered the mirrors. I sank into the tub like a piece of butter on mashed potatoes. I hadn't had a bath since I was a little girl, and I could feel knots in my back melting away. I scrubbed my hair with shampoo that smelled like lavender and thyme, washing away years of anxiety. The bed was a cloud that carried me off to sleep as soon as I tucked myself under the crisp white sheets. I didn't know where I was, or why I was here, but I felt more at peace than I'd ever felt before.

* * *

I awoke to the smell of coffee. I reached for my lego necklace, suddenly frantic when my fingers scraped against my bare collarbone. I threw the blankets back and searched the room until I spotted it on the dresser—I'd taken it off last night before sleeping. *Shit, my gloves!* I'd left them in the pile of dirty laundry. I wrung my bare hands, feeling naked without them.

My brain scrambled to make sense of things. How much of yesterday actually happened? Where was I? I only had a few months until I was let out of JDRI, and now everything was ruined. I had to get back. I forced myself to take a deep breath, squeezing away yesterday's ugly memories.

My stomach was rumbling, so I followed the smell of coffee downstairs. I thought it was coming from the kitchen, but the smell led me into a grand dining room with a long wooden table filled with food.

I filled up a plate with pastries, fried eggs, toast with strawberry jam, and washed it down with fresh espresso and orange juice. I scarfed down the food. Part of me felt like it could disappear at any moment, or I'd be caught and punished for eating so well.

"What are you wearing?" Sitri said, coming in the room. He filled a plate up with eggs and sausages. I looked down at the sweats he'd given me last night.

"Um, the only clothes I *have*?"

"Sorry, I forgot to tell you. Check your closet, you should find something more appropriate. Then meet me back here. Able's been waiting for you to wake up."

Back in my room, I found my closet and drawers full of clothes. Almost every garment came in three different sizes—it was like someone robbed a mall and took a selection from every store. There was even a drawer full of underwear, and another full of makeup and accessories. I moved quickly through the dresses and gowns, and turned my nose up at all the pink garments, to find a section of more practical things. I pulled out a pair of dark denim jeans, a black shirt and a soft, burgundy sweater. That's when I noticed my all stars had been replaced by a brand new pair of sneakers. I felt a pang of longing at first, but the soles had been worn through anyway. In another month I would have had to wrap duct-tape around them just to keep them on my feet. The new pair fit satisfyingly well.

The only thing missing were my gloves. I pulled the sleeves of the sweater down to cover my wrists.

Sitri was waiting for me downstairs. I did a little spin for him.

"Happy now?" I asked.

He shrugged. "It'll do."

He led me back to the library, which I was starting to suspect was really just Able's private study. It was empty.

"Wait here," Sitri said. "He'll be back soon."

I let myself explore the room. While small, it opened up as I looked closer—it was filled with fascinating artifacts and antiques, and smelled like fresh tobacco and polished leather. I couldn't believe that just yesterday I'd been at JDRI. My whole life had turned upside down. And I still had no idea who these people were, or what they wanted from me.

I let my fingers run over the spines of the old leather books. One of them felt lighter than the others. Hollow. I pushed on it, and there was a soft click as the bookshelf swung open. My pulse quickened at the discovery of the secret passage. Behind it was a workroom filled with skulls and knives. The skulls were remarkable; there were over a dozen, mounted on the walls. Most of them had horns—a bull, a deer, and others I didn't recognize. Each was carved with intricate decorations and miniature scenes. A wide desk stood in a corner, with a lighted magnifying glass and a half finished piece of work. This one looked like a ram's head, with wide, curving horns. It was surrounded by small razor blades, carving tools and brushes. Looking closely, I could see that built into the curves and decorations were tiny figures. It was some kind of visual story. I wished I knew what it meant.

"Good morning," Able said behind me. I jumped at the sound of his voice, I hadn't heard anyone come in the room. He was wearing black slacks and a blue tailored shirt. Sitri had returned to the room as well. He rolled his eyes, like he was saying *I can't leave you alone for a minute.*

"Less than a day here and you've already uncovered my secrets." He gave me a bemused expression and I blushed, realizing I'd been snooping.

"I'm so sorry," I said, stepping out of the room and shutting the door. "I wasn't snooping. I just—I like books." I gestured lamely at the bookshelf.

"They're amazing. Did you do them?" It was difficult to picture Able bent over the skulls, working on the meticulous detail.

"It's a hobby. A kind of diary, if you will. I record important life events, things that matter to me. Stories I can't forget. Each one takes several years to finish."

I'd been prepared to barge in and force Able to tell me what was going on, but he was not at all what I imagined. I sat down on one of the leather couches unsure how to begin.

"I've been patient," I said finally. "What am I doing here?"

"Of course," Able said, taking a seat across from me. "Let's start simply. What if I told you there was still magic in the world—just a little bit of it. But someone was trying to kill all the magic, so they alone would have the power to rule? And that they built up an army to hunt innocents?"

"I'd say he sounds like an asshole," I said.

Sitri grinned, and Able burst out laughing. I noticed again how perfectly white their teeth were. It was unnerving.

"I think we're going to get along just fine," Able said, his eyes full of warmth. Despite his wrinkles and gray hair, he radiated energy and strength.

"But, that was a hypothetical question, right?" I shifted uncomfortably, pulling on the sleeves of my sweater. "I mean… *magic?*"

"What do you think happens when you touch people, Kaidance?"

My face paled, and I leaned back slightly.

"What do you *see*?"

"Nothing," I said. The lie I'd spent years practicing came to my lips quickly.

Able frowned, then leaned forward and spoke in low voice.

"I understand you've had to hide the truth for a long time, and that nobody has ever really believed you or understood you before. But you can trust me. You are safe here."

I gave him my wide-eyed, innocent look. True, Sitri had rescued me from JDRI, but I didn't have much choice in the matter. And the longer I stayed here, the more trouble I'd be in when I returned. And I had to go back. If not for my parents, then at least for Sarah and Jessie.

"You can't go back," Able said, as if he'd read my mind. "At least not right now. And you don't need to lie to me." He turned on a TV that had been hidden behind a panel. First, we watched a news report about a runaway mental patient, locked up for killing her little brother, who escaped after murdering a guard. Able was right. If I went back now they'd arrest me. I'd be locked up for the rest of my life. Then he turned on the second video. I gasped and clutched the edge of the couch with my fingers. The scene was dark, but I recognized my old room at JDRI. Two little girls were sitting on a bed, late at night. They were whispering, but I could hear every word clearly. *This was impossible.*

"Did you really do it?" younger Jessie said. "Push your brother? You can tell me."

I shook my head. "I tried to save him," I said, sniffling. "But nobody will believe me."

"I believe you," Jessie said. "But how did you know about the car?"

"I saw it. Sometimes... sometimes when I touch people, I see things. Things that haven't happened yet."

Able paused the video and looked at me expectantly.

"How did you get this," I breathed, afraid of the answer.

"We've been watching you for a long time," Able said. "Not just you—our tech wizard, Heph, hacks into every database looking for anything that could suggest supernatural abilities. If we find something, we install surveillance equipment.

Once we're pretty sure a child or person is truly gifted, we'll plan an extraction."

"You've been watching me for eight years, and only *now* decided to save me? Why now? What changed?" I stood up suddenly, hot fury coursing through my veins.

"That conversation is the only evidence we ever found. You never mentioned it again, and we didn't have any proof that you'd actually done anything remarkable," Able said. "But then we caught this on one of the security feeds. Last week."

He showed me another video. A man with the ash-blond hair and tattooed arms. In my bedroom. Smelling my pillow.

"Who is he?" I asked.

"We call them hunters, but they're more like assassins. Our enemy created them. His own private army, to hunt down and kill anybody with traces of the old magic."

"So he really is trying to kill me?" I asked. I hadn't wanted to believe it, even when he was chasing us in the car. I remembered standing with him in the woods, my hands against his warm chest, looking up into his amber colored eyes. The way he'd pushed me back protectively. I hadn't felt like I was in danger then. In fact I felt safe with him. Safer than I did with Sitri.

"He'd probably interrogate you first," Able said. "Torture you. But ultimately, yes, they would want you dead."

"But… why? Why me? I'm not threat to them."

"Your very existence is a threat. You are proof that contradicts the lie our enemy has been telling for thousands of years. If you were an ordinary human, he wouldn't have been interested in you. And the strange thing is, even after discovering your powers, he should have just killed you right away. That's what they usually do. They find children with power and kill them. The younger the better. That leads me to suspect you have something that he wants, or that he wants to use you somehow."

"I was there, in the woods, the night he made contact with you." Sitri said. "His behavior was… unusual. I've never seen a hunter act that way. That's when we decided to pull you out. I brought the kitten as a final test." I touched my arm where the kitten had scratched me. It was raw and sore.

"What do you see when people touch you?" Able's dark brown eyes bored into mine, almost compelling an answer. Could I trust them? Would they really believe me? Or was this some elaborate hoax, invented to make me confess that I was still crazy and should be kept locked up? I was tired of resisting—of lying to the world, and to myself. It would be a relief to tell someone the truth.

"Death," I said finally. "Tragic, violent, bloody death."

8

Able's eyes widened. His face was excited, almost hungry as he reached for my hands. I snatched them away quickly.

"Forgive me," he said, taking a deep breath and clenching his fists together. "I only wanted to see—Sitri told me there's a mark around your wrist. I would like very much to see it."

I frowned, but pulled up my sleeves and showed him the red ring around my wrist, the one I always kept hidden. Able stood and started pacing.

"Sitri, would you excuse us for a moment?"

When Sitri hesitated, Able shot him a dark look. Sitri bowed his head and made a noise I could have sworn was a whimper. He gave me an apologetic glance and slunk out of the room.

"I appreciate you telling me that," Able said when we were alone. "Seeing the future is a very powerful gift. I think I may understand why they're after you. The ability to see when people are going to meet their deaths—few would dare to know the answer. And the questions it raises… is your vision a warning, or a certainty? I hope we'll be able to help you find out."

He walked to his desk and brought out a black gift box tied with a golden ribbon.

"A welcome gift," he said. "Go ahead, open it."

Inside the box were a pair of elegant, dark leather gloves.

"Rabbit skin," he said. "My niece made them. You'll meet her soon."

I pulled on the gloves. They fit perfectly, and were soft but thin. They were so long they almost reached my elbow. I immediately felt more comfortable, as if I had an invisible shield around me. It was my turn to ask questions.

"Is Sitri related to you too?" I asked.

"No. He's more of an old friend. Someone I trust. You can trust him too."

"What is this place?"

"We call it Nevah. It's a sanctuary of sorts, a place where people with powers can be safe."

"From the hunters. And—your enemy," I asked.

He nodded.

"Everybody here has powers... like mine?"

"We all have our own abilities." Able smiled, then pulled out a blade from one of his pockets and slashed it across his palm. He did this so quickly I barely had time to register what was happening. The blood welled up, and he cupped his hand so it wouldn't drip. His other hand put away the knife and pulled out a handkerchief. When he wiped away the blood, I could see that the wound was already starting to heal.

"That's impossible," I said.

Able shrugged. "You may find your ideas of what's possible challenged while you're at

Nevah." He folded up the handkerchief and I watched him tuck it away. I made sure to note what pocket the knife was in as well. Able may look like a kind old gentleman, but he was fast, and dangerous. I couldn't afford to let my guard down.

"Why did you bring me here?" I asked.

"I thought we'd made that clear by now," Able said, looking disappointed. "Someone was trying to kill you, Kaidance. If we hadn't brought you here, you'd probably be dead already."

"But that's not all, is it? What do you want from me?" If I'd learned one thing at JDRI, it was that people didn't help you for no reason. I felt more comfortable knowing what it was right away.

"Before we get to that, we need to figure out who you are, and what you can do. You've always had to hide and repress your powers. Here we want you to embrace them. You'll practice, challenge yourself, and see what you're really capable of."

"To what end? So you can use me? So I'll join your war?"

"We'll never force you to do anything you don't want to do," Able said. "But if, after getting to know us, you believe our cause is just, then you would be welcome to join us."

"And if not? Am I a prisoner here?"

"Now that is an interesting question," Able said. "I'd like to say that you can leave anytime you want. If the hunters weren't after you, you could just go back to JDRI, and probably be imprisoned for the rest of your life. We feel that would be unfortunate. But since the hunters *are* after you, I have to ask myself what they want with you. Maybe they have a plan that involves you. Maybe they will use you to destroy this place, and kill all of my friends and family—not to mention the thousands of souls in my care and under my protection. Do you see my dilemma?"

"I'd never kill anybody," I said.

"Never say never, Dear. And the other side wouldn't let you make that choice. They would do whatever it takes to win. Compulsion, orders, punishment and pain. Not free will. At any rate, this is all hypothetical until we actually know more about you, so I propose we table this discussion for a week. You can relax and get to know us. Attend some of the classes and activities, meet with some of our specialists, and then we'll decide on the best course of action together. If you still want to go back to JDRI, back to your old life, I'll help you. I might even be able to exonerate you from that nasty murder charge, and you can have a relatively normal life again. Does that sound fair?"

I was still skeptical, but it did sound like a good offer. Without Able's help, I'd be facing jail or worse. And I was in no hurry to give up my new bed and the amazing food. Plus, I was curious. Able was treating me like I had a gift—a talent even. Something of value, rather than simply the awful, destructive curse I've always considered it to be.

"I have one condition," I said. "I need to get a letter to my friends and parents. Just to tell them I'm okay."

Able smiled, "I believe Heph can help you with that. I'll have Sitri take you down."

I nodded self-consciously. I wasn't sure if we should shake on it or something, but Able made no move towards me. I got up and turned to leave.

"Just one more thing," Able said quietly. "Your gift, as special as it is, might make some people uncomfortable. If everybody knew what you could do, I don't doubt you'd have a hundred people lined up outside your door, hoping to see where they meet their doom. For their sakes, and for your own privacy, I would request you keep that secret between us. Use the gloves, and keep your hands and wrists covered, so we don't have any incidences."

"What should I tell them?" I asked.

"Tell them you see visions of the future sometimes, but that you can't control it, and I've forbidden you to try and read anybody's fortune. You can say it's because we don't want you to mess up your training, which we take very seriously."

Sitri was waiting just outside the door. I wondered if he'd been listening in. Able told him to take me to Heph so I could send some messages, then closed the door behind us.

"What the hell is Able?" I whispered as we moved down the hallway. "He cut his hand and then it was just fine, like nothing happened."

"There are two kinds of people here," Sitri said. "Immortals and heirs."

"Immortals, seriously? Like, they live forever?"

"Let's just say that nobody has been able to kill them yet, and they won't die natural deaths of old age. The immortals are mostly related to Able somehow. So it's a little like a royal dynasty. They run this place. And they're very powerful."

"And the heirs?" I asked.

"The heirs are humans who have inherited certain genes or traits. Usually the descendants of immortals. So they have some power—a reflection of whatever bloodline they have in them, and how many generations down the line they are. But normal, otherwise."

"Normal," I snorted. "Like me?" I held up my hands, which were covered to the elbow with the dark leather gloves. "Wait—what are *you*?" I asked.

Sitri gave me wicked grin, flashing his teeth.

"I'm something else." He pushed the doors open into another room, and I gasped as we went inside. It was a large hall filled with computer screens and high tech equipment. It seemed out of place in a building filled with classical decorations.

"It looks like you could launch rockets from in here," I said.

"You can," Sitri said with a smirk. We walked past several rows of empty stations, to a circular area in the center of the room. That's when I noticed the room was already occupied.

"This is Mist, Dion, and Heph," Sitri said, pointing them out one by one. "I hope we aren't interrupting."

"Nah man," Dion said. "Join the party!" He grabbed a couple of paper cups and started pouring from an unmarked bottle. "You've got to try this one. Just opened. Made in 1832, and it's finally starting to taste pretty good." Despite his dark skin, I could still see the flush in Dion's cheeks. I guessed he'd had more than a few cups already. He had dark eyes and long brown hair like a musketeer. Middle Eastern maybe, or just really tan.

"Speaking of things that taste good, who's this delicious little morsel?" Dion ran his eyes over my body. It was my turn to blush. I might have been creeped out, if he wasn't so good looking. The sparkle in his eyes let me know he was just teasing, but I felt Sitri tense beside me. For a second I pictured him throwing Dion across the room, defending my honor.

"Able's new toy," Mist said, frowning at me. "Careful Sitri, or he'll replace you with her." Mist had the build of a ballerina and was wearing jeans and a mustard colored sweater. Her face was free from makeup, and perfectly symmetrical, accentuating her large brown eyes and thick lashes. She reminded me of a deer; even the nimble way she'd jumped up when we entered.

"Ah, that'll never happen," Dion said, standing up and putting an arm around Sitri. "Sitri's been loyal to our family all these years. He's irreplaceable. Right Heph?"

Heph was on the computer with large earphones on and his back to us. It didn't seem like he'd even noticed us come in.

"I'm going for a run," Mist said, tying her hair back in a ponytail. "Dion, you should find someone to screw, you're getting bawdy again."

"How about it, darling?" Dion said, grabbing my gloved hand, and reaching another behind me. This time Sitri reacted, catching Dion by the wrist and pulling him away from me. "Easy there tiger," he said. "It's her first day, and her dance card is full. Able wants her to start training."

Mist rolled her eyes. "She's as skinny as a twig. Apart from her pomegranates, which look ripe enough. I could break her in half over my leg."

Dion smirked. "I'd like to break her in half over my—"

"Sitri!" Heph said, finally noticing us. He smiled and removed his earphones. His long, curly hair fell to the sides of his scruffy goatee. "Oh, are you guys still here?" he said, looking at Dion and Mist. His sage green eyes matched his olive skin.

"Just leaving," Dion said. "Thanks for the good times. Oh and here," he handed the bottle to Heph.

"You finish this one, I'll get another."

"Sorry about that," Sitri said when they'd left. "Dion comes on a little strong."

"I noticed," I said. Actually I thought the exchange was kind of funny. I could handle myself with a guy like Dion. And at least he was friendly. Mist, on the other hand, seemed to genuinely dislike me.

"You shouldn't antagonize him," Heph said to Sitri. "I mean I know he seems like a tipsy manwhore, but a lot of it is an act. He's smart. And he can be vicious. I mean unless she's already yours—"

"Excuse me?" I snapped. "I'm not anybody's. I just don't like people touching me."

"Okay, got it," Heph said, raising his hands up in mock defense. "What can I do for you two?"

"Able said you could help me send some messages," I said.

"Sure. Text? Email?"

"Letters. By mail."

"Why don't you just use smoke signals?" He smirked.

"Can you do it or not?" I snapped. Everybody seemed so relaxed here, it was easy to forget my whole life had just been uprooted, not to mention a man killed. I couldn't stand the thought of Sarah and Jessie thinking I'd done it. And I was getting tired of all the joking around.

I thought Heph was going to get angry or say something clever, but he just turned back to his computer with a hurt expression. He pulled up a blank document, then got up so I could take his seat.

"Type whatever you want to send, then the names and addresses. I'll put in an order to a post office on the other side of the country, they'll print it out and ship it. It'll be there by tomorrow. Completely untraceable."

Good enough. I wrote short letters to Sarah and Jessie, telling them I wasn't in danger and would try to come back soon—and also that I hadn't killed Dennis, so they shouldn't believe the news. Then I tried writing a letter to my parents. They'd probably heard by now that I'd escaped. But they'd never believe me over the official report. They hadn't last time. My chest tightened as I stared at the blank document. Maybe it was too early to write to them. Able said he'd help me get my own life back. If he could really do that, maybe it would cause my parents less worry and heartbreak not to hear from me at all. They'd moved on with their lives years ago, maybe I needed to move on with mine.

"I'm done. Just those two," I said finally, standing up.

"You sure?" Sitri said.

"It's fine," I said. "I don't know what to say anyway. Now what?"

"Now we start training, and find out what makes you so special."

9

Sitri led me upstairs to the third floor of the building and into a spacious room with dark wood furniture. In the back of the room was a table full of vases and freshly cut flowers. A woman with her back to us was making an arrangement of lilies.

"This is Stephanie," he said, as the woman turned around to greet us. "Able's wife."

I tried to hide the shock on my face but failed miserably. She looked *way* too young for Able. I would have guessed fifteen.

"Why don't you run along and let Kaidance and I get to know each other," she said to Sitri. He nodded and left the room without looking at me.

She had long, black hair, and her cornflower blue eyes sparkled like sapphires. She was wearing a long white dress, with a wreath of pink and white flowers. I could tell by the floral scent that they were real. For some reason, I thought she looked like a virgin bride about to be sacrificed.

"My husband tells me I'm to help you with your gift," she said.

I hesitated. Able said I shouldn't talk about my powers.

"You can see death," Stephanie said, smiling knowingly. "Able and I tell each other everything, but I would have been able to see that about you anyway."

When she smiled, her face lit up like the spring. But there was a touch of sadness in her eyes, and she moved with a gravitas that suggested she was far older than she looked. She gestured to a small table and I sat down as she poured me a cup of tea, in an antique teacup with oriental designs.

"How could you have seen that?" I asked.

"Let's say death and I have a very close relationship. Able said you may have the ability to see the future. He's curious what else you can do."

"Why would I be able to do anything else?" I took a sip of my tea, and tasted chamomile and rose petals.

"Powers can manifest in many different ways. The magic is in the blood, but defined by the person. It's kind of like how different blacksmiths can make a variety of swords with the same metal."

"What are your powers?" I asked.

Stephanie went to the window and opened the latch to an ornate birdcage. She took out one of the little birds. Its dark feathers had a purple sheen in the light. She held it up to me on the palm of her hand, then squished it in her fist—tearing into its little body with her fingernails. The bird and I cried out in unison. I reached out to grab the bird away from her, but when she opened her hand again, it was already dead, and her palm was smeared with blood. She took my hand and pulled off one of my gloves, then placed the bird in my hand.

"If you had touched this bird a moment ago," she said, "you might have seen me crush it. You would have seen its end. But you wouldn't have seen this."

She placed her hands over mine. I felt a warmth, and movement on my palm—the scratching of tiny talons. When she removed her hand, the bird was standing on my palm, looking dazed.

"You can bring things back to life," I said. The jealousy tore me to the core. Here was a useful power. The power to restore. To *save*. If only I'd had a power like that. The chunk of legos around my neck felt heavy, a burden of guilt and regret.

"It's easier with animals." She shrugged and put the bird back in its cage. "Men are different. If the body dies, the soul goes somewhere else. Even if you bring the body back, it won't be the same person, not unless you retrieve the soul as well."

She squeezed my shoulder. Her ice blue gaze reached deep inside me, and I knew she was talking about my brother. "But life and death, it's mainly just animating force. Life needs a will to survive. The will to exist, to fight. If it has that, it will usually figure the rest out. If it doesn't, nothing can save it. I can remove that will."

The room darkened as though a large cloud was passing over the window. In the pale light, Stephanie suddenly looked terrifying. The flowers around her head dried up and withered.

The skirts of her dress and the tips of her hair writhed around her like serpents caught in an invisible wind, and I could have sworn she was getting taller—until I saw her feet had left the ground.

And that's when I felt it. A powerful despair. A hopelessness that consumed my whole being. It reminded me of my dark phase at JDRI, but worse. My bones felt like melting wax, and I stumbled. I put a hand out on the back of a chair for stability. Then the light came back, and I was myself again, in this bright and pleasant little room. I felt a drip of sweat glide down my forehead.

"You're stronger than you look," Stephanie said, arching one eyebrow.

"You too," I smiled weakly.

"That routine sometimes turns grown men into sniveling cowards."

"I don't doubt it."

"Well then," she said, "now that that's over, let's go for a walk, shall we?"

Stephanie knocked on a door down the hall. I took a sharp breath when it opened and Mist peered out at us. She scowled when she saw me. I wasn't happy to see her either. *I thought Stephanie was helping me find my powers?*

"Kaidance and I need some help," she said. "Got a minute?"

"I'm kind of busy—" Mist said at first, but a sharp look from Stephanie changed her attitude.

"Fine," she said with a sigh. She shrugged on a suede jacket. I noticed again how beautiful she was. Her light brown hair was parted in the middle and tucked behind her delicate ears. She was wearing tight navy jeans and a pair of lightweight sneakers. She looked like a posh Englishwoman about to go for a horse ride.

I did a double take when we emerged from the back entrance of the ground floor. The sprawling manor was built on top of the crumbling remains of what looked like an ancient temple. Statues were built into the walls, which were supported by towering pillars. They protruded from the modern building like ribs from a massive rotting corpse. Facing the temple was a large half circle of red dirt, surrounded by ascending staircases which were built into the hill. It was an amphitheater. *In Washington State.*

"This is impossible," I said. "I mean, it's a replica, right?" Able had said my ideas of what's possible would be challenged, but this flew in the face of everything I knew about human civilization. Even after what I'd just seen Stephanie do, somehow this was harder for my brain to accept.

Mist rolled her eyes at me, making me feel stupid.

"It's real," Stephanie said. "We came here thousands of years ago. We modernize the house every century or so, but we kept the ruins pretty much as they are. It makes us feel at home."

"You mean, your *people* came here, right?"

"Can we save the history lessons for another time?" Mist said. "Let's get this over with. What do you need me to do?"

"Just shoot some arrows at her," said Stephanie.

Wait, what? My heart started pounding and I almost tripped over my own feet. Mist flashed me a dangerous grin.

"No way," I said. "She'll kill me."

"She's an exceptional shot," Stephanie said. "She won't kill you unless she does it on purpose. And she won't do that because I'm asking her not to."

"Is this really necessary?" I asked.

"You don't know what your powers are or how to summon them," Stephanie said. "But that's not a problem you can solve by thinking. I could make you sit and meditate for eight hours a day, but that's boring, and rarely works. Trust me, we've tried it that way. No, it's so much faster to put you in mortal danger. Get your adrenaline pumping. Remember, all life wants is to survive. When your body feels threatened, when it's desperate to defend itself, that's when you'll have a breakthrough."

I was skeptical, but I let Stephanie lead me towards a stack of hay bales and position me in front of them. "You're going to want to stay very, very still," she whispered, then kissed me on the cheek. I gulped. A cold breeze tickled my arms, and I shivered.

Mist stood about fifty feet away from me, holding a simple wooden bow. She nocked an arrow and drew back the string. My heart started pounding. "Ready?" she called.

Just as I opened my mouth to reply, an arrow sunk into the hay bale behind me, so close the fletching ripped a gash in my left ear. My ear throbbed in pain. I reached up to touch it, and my fingers came away red with blood. I was tempted to run back inside to find Able or Sitri, but I didn't want to let Mist know that she'd scared me.

"I thought you said she wouldn't hurt me," I said to Stephanie, who was standing on the other side of the small wooden fence surrounding the area.

"I said she wouldn't *kill* you," Stephanie said, but she gave Mist a warning look.

The next arrow came right between my legs, thwacking against the hay bale and my right thigh. I cried out in surprise. I was definitely going to have a bruise there later. This was crazy.

"Should I be doing anything?" I asked.

"Focus on your attacker. Focus on the arrows. See them coming towards you. Stop them."

"But how?" I asked.

Stephanie shrugged. "Any way you can."

I took a deep breath and tried to focus. Another arrow went just under my armpit, between my body and my arm. My right arm snapped out in reflex as the arrow bit into my flesh, and as it did I felt another slide between my fingers. I realized that Mist had shot an arrow between my fingers *while my arm was moving*. My heart was already pounding, but for the first time I felt really scared, thinking of all the places Mist could put an arrow without actually killing me.

That's when I realized the last arrow hadn't finished moving. The others had buried into the hay bale so quickly I barely saw them fly past me. But this one I could feel, gliding between my fingers smoothly. I brought my awareness to it just as time sped up and the fletching tore a chunk out of my index finger. Blood gushed out of the wound, and my mask of strength failed me. The places where the arrows had hit were screaming in pain. *I didn't ask to be tortured like this.* Tears of frustration started welling up in my eyes. Stephanie held up a hand for Mist to stop, then came onto the field.

She took a long band of fabric from her pocket and wound it tightly around my injured finger.

"Anything?" she asked.

I shook my head.

"Oh well, it was worth a shot," she said, with her signature sad smile. I realized Stephanie might be a bit mad.

"Are we done?" I asked.

"One more thing," she nodded to Mist, who leaned her bow against the fence with a smug smile. Then she took off her jacket and started walking towards us.

"We do a lot of combat training here," Stephanie said. "For exercise, for fun, and because we have a lot of time on our hands and get bored."

"You want us to fight?" I said, my mouth hanging open.

"Ridiculous, right?" Mist said, her lips curling up into lopsided smile. "I'd get more resistance from a punching bag."

"You don't *have* to do this," Stephanie said. "I won't ever ask you to do something against your will. I won't force you. But if you want to learn to control your powers, this is the best way I know how to teach you."

"What if I see something?" I asked in a hushed voice. I still had my gloves on, but if Mist hit my face it could still trigger a vision.

"I doubt you will," she said, "but if you do, tell me afterwards. In private."

I nodded. It beat standing still and getting shot at. Besides, I could fight. Jessie taught me a few moves. She made me practice throwing punches until my arms ached. I put my fists up in front of my face, in the defensive position she'd showed me.

Mist laughed, then ducked and swept my legs out from under me with a low kick that put me on my back. I rolled on the ground, gasping for air. I noticed that we had a few watchers now. Sitri stood just outside the fence, his arms crossed, looking angry. And there were several others I didn't recognize.

I pushed myself to my feet. This time I started bouncing on the balls of my feet, moving back and forth. *Keep moving,* Jessie would shout at me. *Don't let them see it coming*. But Mist was as nimble as a rabbit. I threw jabs and punches, but she ducked and spun between them. I didn't see her fist until it was an inch from my eye. Then an explosion of pain, and I was on my back again. I groaned and pushed myself up, coughing on the cloud of dust I'd made when I hit the ground. There were more people watching now. This was embarrassing. But what did they expect? Mist was obviously well-trained, and I'd never been in a real fight in my life.

"Any tips?" I yelled at Sitri.

"Stop falling down," he said.

I glared at him.

"Stay on your feet. Watch her shoulders. Take the punch and hit back anyway."

I took a few more hits before I figured out what he meant. The muscles of her shoulder would flex just before she threw a punch. I saw the next punch coming. Time seemed to slow as I concentrated on her shoulder. Instead of ducking, I flailed out with my hand, swinging at her wildly. Her punch hit me square on the jaw and snapped my head backward, but not before my palm hit her cheek with a slap that echoed in the amphitheater. I heard a few claps and cheers from the audience.

Mist came at me again, newly enraged. Still reeling from the last punch, I couldn't even lift my arms to defend myself as she hit me with a flurry of punches, followed by a kick in the stomach that sent me flying backwards. I landed like a bag of bones. Every part of my body was in agony. I lay in the dirt, drool hanging out of my mouth, one eye swelling shut from that first punch.

Get up. I told myself. Get UP.

But my body wasn't working. Instead it shut down. That's when my vision blurred and I saw the golden thread. I thought it was a bit of blond hair, and wondered where it came from, since both Mist and I were brunette. The way it moved seemed unnatural. It drifted slowly in front of my vision. And it was *long*. Without moving my head I couldn't see an end to it on either side. My fingers twitched, and I had an urge to reach out and touch it. But before I could, exhaustion overcame me, and I blacked out.

10

I blinked my eyes frantically and gulped in air. Sitri had one arm around me and was practically carrying me back into the house. I must have only been out a few minutes. He breathed a sigh of relief when I opened my eyes. “They shouldn’t have done that to you,” he said, his voice shaking. “Mist is a trained warrior, there’s hardly anyone here who could give her a fair fight.”

“Stephanie wanted me to fail,” I mumbled. My jaw felt like it wasn’t connected properly. It clicked when I talked. I tried to move my legs, to take some of my weight off Sitri, but they felt like jelly. I relaxed against Sitri's powerful chest, breathing in the smell of him. We stumbled into a wing of the house connected by a side entrance. It had big glass windows and rows of plants. In the center was a fountain with a pool of crystal clear water, surrounding a statue of a man with a beard and a toga. He was holding a staff with a snake climbing up it.

"My, what have we here?" said a woman with long red hair. She set down a tin watering can near the fountain, and grabbed a basket full of medical supplies instead. She was a little older than me, maybe mid-twenties, but like almost everybody here, had a youthful glow. Her eyes were slate gray. Sitri laid me down on a thin bed with crisp white sheets, and I realized this must be an infirmary of sorts.

"This is Alice," Sitri said.

"Let me guess," I said, mumbling through my thick lip. "You have some magic healing abilities?"

"I've never liked the word magic, personally," Alice said. "Let's just say I've been around a long time, and have an exceptional amount of medicinal wisdom. Things may seem like magic to you because you can't understand why they're working, but everything I do is obviously within the bounds of physical possibility."

"Obviously?" I said. "Nothing that has happened to me in the last few days seems obvious. And Able showed me his neat super-healing trick. You're telling me that's explainable?"

"Sure," Alice said. "Our bodies are made up of cells. They are built to restore and repair injuries." She poured a few drops of oil from a glass vial onto a cotton swab, and started wiping it against the cut on my ear. I gritted my teeth against the burn.

"Certain, *individuals*," she continued, "merely have an excess of energy. An abundance. So the things that take your body a week, only take them a few seconds, because they can draw on a source of energy that most of us don't have access to." She wrapped my ear with white gauze and taped it into a bandage.

"So the immortals just have more energy somehow?" I asked.

“Most of them come from a much earlier time, when there were fewer living beings,” Alice said, starting on my arm. “Higher consciousness beings take up more energy. In the beginning, there were a few dozen of them; then hundreds; then thousands. Today there are *billions*, and when they’re born they divide the available amount of universal energy equally between them. Which means, most humans these days only get a tiny bit of it. Heirs are descendants of powerful beings who were made with more energy. It gets diminished with each generation, but it’s still more than most regular people get. But immortals—especially the early ones—they may have as much energy as a billion living humans. Take him, for example,” she said, nodding at the statue.

“Asclepius, god of medicine. Son of Apollo. He set up sanctuaries to teach the healing arts. Just being near ordinary humans, or charging the pools with his energy, was enough to dramatically speed their healing.”

“Sounds great. He still around?” I joked. Sitri and Alice shared a look. “Unfortunately, no,”

Alice said finally. "But we'll do the best we can without him."

"That's why they did it, you know," Sitri said darkly. "It wasn't just about getting you to use your powers. They wanted to hurt you, to see how fast you'd heal. It's one way to figure out how powerful you are."

"It's pretty common, actually," Alice said. "Almost everybody ends up in here the first day. I mean, it's not exactly hazing—but it does help speed up the process."

"What process?" I asked.

"You can't start improving your abilities until you know what they are, and what you can do. Part of that is knowing which bloodline you have, who you are related to."

"Can't they just use DNA testing or something?"

Alice laughed, "I've been trying to get Able to do exactly that for the past decade. But he's worried about putting our genetic DNA markers in a database, even something secure, which I'm sure Heph would have no trouble making. Able is more traditional. If you want to keep a secret, don't write it down."

"Well, I think in this case, they're going to be disappointed," I said.

"Why?" Sitri asked.

I held up my index finger to show them the angry wound that was still oozing blood.

"It's been fifteen minutes and I still feel like shit."

Alice gave me a tea made of fresh herbs. I sipped on the steaming cup, trying to ignore the throbbing pain in my cut finger, my thigh, my ear—and the pounding headache raging behind my swollen eye. The tea relaxed me. I felt my limbs become heavy.

When I lay back against the pillows, my body felt like it was floating. Alice put a warm poultice over my eye and bandaged up all my cuts and sores with something that felt cool and tingly. I smelled tea tree and lavender oil, mixed with something bitter I couldn't place. Then my arms got heavy, like stones, and I couldn't move my fingers, and then I was gone.

I was back in the meadow on the hilltop. The limbs of the tree swayed gently in the breeze. A falling leaf brushed against my arm. The deer was gone, but the goat was still munching away. I rubbed my hands over his back and felt the soft, curly white hair. I could smell lavender and oregano. It was so peaceful here. I felt like nothing could hurt me.

I waited for one of the women to come up like they had before, but no one came. After a few minutes I decided to look for them. I followed the path down the hill and came to the mouth of the cave. The entrance was dark, but I had an urge to enter anyway and see where it led. I walked down a set of staircases that had been carved directly into the rock, keeping one hand against the cool wall of the tunnel. At the bottom of the steep decline, the path opened into a large cavern. Light streamed down from holes in the rock far above; it shone like a spotlight on the almost domestic scene. Three women were doing chores. One pulled up water from an old well made of large stones. Another was digging white clay from the walls with a sharp spade, and the third was spinning wool into thread on an old-fashioned spinning wheel. None of them looked up when I entered. They kept working, their repetitive motions creating a soothing rhythm—a machine-like hum.

I approached the well in the center of the cavern. The surface was so smooth and clear I could see my reflection. Suddenly another face came into view—the same old woman that had seen me last time. I whirled around to face her.

"Cut the thread," she said. "Save the tree."

Then she shoved me. I went flailing backwards over the rim of the well and fell into darkness.

When I woke up again, it was dark and I was alone. I felt a little groggy, but most of the pain had subsided to a dull ache. I found my gloves on a table nearby and pulled them on, wincing as they disturbed the gauze on my finger. Then I walked past the fountain and found the stairs. I heard voices and followed them to the grand dining room where I'd had breakfast. Silver candlesticks illuminated the table, which was covered by a satin red cloth. They mirrored the glowing chandeliers above the table, under which most of the family had already gathered.

I looked first for Sitri but didn't see him. Besides Heph, Mist, Dion, Stephanie, Alice and Able, there was another girl across from Mist, and a younger boy I didn't recognize sitting next to Able. Stephanie was at the head of the table with her husband. I didn't want to interrupt and was thinking of just going to bed without eating.

"Ah, there you are," Able said, spotting me just as I was about to retreat to my room. "I see you've survived the afternoon. Take a seat and join us." Alice gave me a warm smile.

The only empty chair was across the length of the table, at the other head. I didn't make a move towards it. I noticed that they were all dressed up. Not in dresses and suits, exactly, but a certain elegant chic that they wore so casually it hadn't registered at first. I looked down at my dirty, bloodstained and torn clothes.

"I'm not hungry," I lied, eyeing the plates full of roast beef, chicken, vegetables, bread and potatoes. Silver dishes held gravy and butter. My stomach rumbled.

Able turned and said something to the boy next to him. He sprang up and grabbed a chair from against the wall nearby, and slid it into place next to him. Then he pulled it out for me and smiled. *Cute kid.*

I sat in the chair and thanked him. He nodded, his golden blond curls shining in the dim light. Alice gave me a little wave from across the table.

"Let's see, who haven't you met?" Able said.

"I introduced her to my fists not long ago," Mist said, smirking. "It looks like she and them didn't get along."

Able frowned at her and tapped his fingers against the table. His rings sparkled in the candlelight. Mist flashed him a look and went silent.

"I'm Tori," said the girl across from Mist, leaning around Dion and nodding at me with a small smile. She had darker skin than the others, and a sultry, bedroom voice. Indian I guessed. Her cleavage was practically spilling out of the pink sweat suit she was wearing. Her puffy round lips had a small gap between them that I wanted to put my finger in.

What the fuck is wrong with me?

I tore my gaze away, my cheeks flaming. I'd never been into girls, but something about Tori had me captivated. Out of the corner of my eye I saw her smile and exchange looks with Dion. He leaned over and filled my wineglass from a green bottle.

The boy next to me was called Sam. He looked a few years younger than me—about the same age my brother would have been. Like everybody else at the table, Sam had perfectly symmetrical features, which made him look slightly inhuman. Like a porcelain cherub. The roughest looking at the table was Heph, with his scruffy goatee and long hair, but he wasn't hard to look at. He had a low cut T-shirt that showed off a bit of his bronze chest, and some wooden beads around his neck. If he was trying to look unkempt, it wasn't working. He just looked like a hot surfer.

Heph's skin wasn't as dark as Tori's, but noticeable compared to Able, Stephanie and Mist, who were all—incredibly—paler than I was. I was pale like you could see through my skin. Fragile, translucent. Their skin was pale like marble statues, thick and smooth.

As I piled my plate up with food, I wondered how they were related, if at all. Had Able said Mist was his niece? If Stephanie was Able's husband, could she be someone's *mother*? Apart from Sam, she looked like the youngest one at the table.

"Why is she even here, anyway?" I heard Mist say in a whisper that carried. "I thought this was a *family* dinner. And what's with the gloves?"

I looked at Able for help. Mist was being rude, but it didn't seem to bother anyone else. Instead they all looked at Able expectantly, like they'd been wondering the same thing.

"Kaidance might have the ability to see the future," Able said. There was a moment of total silence as everyone else stopped eating.

"That's a useful trick," Dion said,

Mist crossed her arms and scowled at me.

"It isn't common?" I asked.

"No," Stephanie said. "The future has always been mysterious, even among immortals. When humans have the gift of sight, they're often related to Prometheus or Apollo."

"You know the story of Cassandra, don't you?" Alice asked, just when I'd taken a big bite of food.

"Could tell the future, but nobody believed her. Right?" I mumbled.

"Do you know how it happened? Apollo gave her the gift of prophecy in order to seduce her, but she later refused him. So he cursed her, so she wouldn't be believed."

"That bitch deserved it," Mist spat. "She had no right refusing him. She was one of his priestesses, working in a temple of Apollo. She was one of Apollo's Sacred Virgins. When she signed up they told her she needed to keep herself pure for Apollo. Did she think he wasn't actually going to come and claim what was his? If so, then she was never a true believer."

"But she had kids," Alice continued. "So her blood is fairly common. Different people see different glimpses of the future, in different ways. Not all of them useful."

"And Prometheus?" I asked, taking a sip of wine.

"Prometheus means foresight," Able said. "People used to consider him their savior. When the world was being made, the gods screwed up dividing rations, and humans were left with nothing. So Prometheus gave them a little bit of fire he stole from the forges of Olympus, and technology."

"That's never been proven," Heph said, raising a finger with a crease in his brow.

"Could he really see the future?" I asked.

"I think it might be more appropriate," Able said, "to say he was supremely well informed."

"One time the king of Arcadia sacrificed a boy to Zeus," Sam said, his eyes excited. "Zeus didn't like it, so he unleashed a deluge, and the rivers ran in torrents and the sea flooded the coastal plain, engulfed the foothills with spray, and washed everything clean. But Prometheus told his son, Deucalion, to build a great wooden chest and fill it with provisions. So humanity was saved."

"Wait—isn't that the story of Noah and the Ark?" I asked.

"Which story do you think came first?" Dion said, smirking.

"It's exactly the kind of thing Zeus would do," Able said, his features hardening. "He let people sacrifice children to him for thousands of years. Then one day he decided it was bad for his image, or cruel, or something. So he decided to just kill everybody and start over. If Prometheus hadn't saved Deucalion, the humans would have been exterminated."

"Deucalion founded the first cities and raised the first temples after the flood," Alice said.

"Temples to *Zeus*," Mist corrected. "Prometheus knew Zeus would just try to kill them again when he found out. So he told Deucalion to build a temple and *thank* Zeus for sparing them, which was total bullshit. But it worked. Zeus liked the look of that temple. He liked humans bowing down and groveling in front of him. So he helped them repopulate. He told them to throw stones over their shoulders and where they fell, they became men and women."

Stones that became men and women? This was obviously just mythology. Why were we even talking about this stuff?

"So," I said, polishing off my plate, "you think I'm related to Apollo or Prometheus?"

Mist snorted. "Not likely. She's a total wimp. I mean, just look at what I did to her face. And she doesn't seem that smart either." I reached a hand up to my face. My eye was still swollen. I hadn't checked myself in a mirror yet, and realized I probably had a black eye. I could withstand Mist's bullying, but sitting with this group of people that looked like movie stars, when I looked like I'd been through hell, made me too self-conscious to deal. Besides, I'd already finished eating. I didn't need to be here.

"Excuse me," I said, pushing away from the table. I didn't look back as I left the room, and nobody stopped me. Back in my room I checked out my face in the vanity mirror. My eye looked like a bruised plum. I touched it gingerly. I tugged off my gloves, then took off all the bandaids. *Holy shit.* My eyes widened. I had dark stitches all over. Two in my left ear, seven under my right arm and four on the inside of my index finger. I looked like Frankenstein. Those arrows had cut me deep. I also had a bruise the size of a grapefruit on my thigh. At least the bleeding had stopped.

I smelled rank, so I stripped off all my dirty clothes and wrapped a towel around me. When I went into the bathroom, I just about ran into Sitri. He was shaving, wearing low cut jeans and nothing else. I pulled the towel tighter against my body.

"I'll be out in a minute," he said, without looking at me. My eyes were drawn to his stomach muscles. They were so hard he looked like a plastic action figure. I wanted to throw off the white towel and tackle him with my mouth, but I couldn't get a read on him—not that I had any experience with boys.

"Why weren't you at dinner?" I asked.

"I stopped eating dinner at the house ages ago," he said. "Got tired of all the reminiscing. Plus I'm not really family."

"Are they all related to each other?" I asked.

"Pretty much. But it's complicated."

I nodded, watching the way his biceps rippled every time he raised the razor to his cheek.

"Ok, I'm done," he said, wiping his face off with a towel.

"Sitri," I said as he turned to go. I closed the gap between us, until I was looking up into his eyes.

"Thank you for saving me," I said. It was a risk, being all up in his personal space, but I wanted to get a reaction from him. I wanted him to notice me.

He smelled like soap and aftershave. He reached down and tucked my hair behind my ear. I thought maybe he was going to kiss me. But instead, he just examined the stitches for a second. "Alice can take those out tomorrow," he said. Then went back to his room and closed the door.

I couldn't sleep that night. All I could think about was how Able must have made a mistake. Compared to the things I'd seen Able and Stephanie do, my powers didn't seem like anything special. Mist certainly didn't think I deserved to be here. And according to Alice, the angry bruises all over my body proved I didn't have a lot of immortal blood in me. Able must have been disappointed to see me at dinner. I hadn't wanted to come to Nevah at all, but now I was worried about being forced to leave.

What would happen if I wasn't what they were looking for? Would they take me back to JDRI? Would I be locked up again? I remember Puriel's determined expression as he chased us on his bike—if they made me go back, it wouldn't take long for him to catch up to me. And I had no way of defending myself against him. Would Sitri and Able just abandon me now, once they figured out I didn't have whatever it was they needed?

The sounds of people having sex broke through my cyclic pessimism. At first I thought it was Sitri, and my heart ached. *Of course* he would already have a girlfriend here. With girls like Tori and Mist around, I'm not surprised he didn't even look at me. But when I snuck into the bathroom and put my ear against his door, it was quiet. The noise was coming from outside my main door.

Out in the hall it was louder. I recognized Tori's voice. Her moans were so loud she was practically screaming. Did they seriously not care that everybody could hear them? I found the door the noise was coming from, and saw light coming out from under it. I was sweating now, from the fear of being discovered. I should go back to my room. Instead, hating myself for it, I bent down and looked through the old fashioned keyhole, which was just large enough to make out the scene inside the room. Tori on black satin sheets, being rammed by Dion—or at last I'm pretty sure it was Dion, he was wearing a mask that looked like it was laughing.

A floorboard creaked behind me, loud enough that Dion and Tori stopped and looked straight at the door. *At me.* My heart jumped through my chest, and I ran down the hall as quietly as I could.

I pushed forward, turning corners blindly until I was far away from the room, then sank down against the wall. *Had someone seen me?* The thought of someone watching me, while I was peeping through the keyhole like a psycho, made my cheeks burn with shame. When I finally caught my breath, I realized I was in a wing of the building I hadn't been in before. A soft blue light was coming from under a door at the end of the hall.

I wasn't sure it was safe to go back to my room yet, so I decided to check it out. I gasped when I opened the door. Inside was a room the size of a basketball court, filled with a full-sized replica of a Greek temple. Probably the Parthenon, from the pictures I'd seen of it. Massive statues of the gods of Olympus stood on alcoves that surrounded the room.

The floor was an enormous mosaic, and in the center of the room was a tree with golden leaves. I stepped forward and could see Greek characters carved into the tree branches and leaves. They glowed with blue light. Lines were cut into the floor filled with the same glowing substance. They flowed like little rivers from the statues towards the tree. In the quiet of the hall, I thought I could hear breathing. Paranoid, I checked over all the statues again, but they didn't flinch.

I stepped to the side of the tree and saw the statue of Zeus, in the center against the far wall. I could tell it was him because he was holding a bolt of lightning. The lines from him to the tree were much bigger and brighter than the others, and I could see that he had fathered lines that went up and wrapped around the tree. The majority of the branches were tied to him in some way. This was a living family tree of some kind. But that wasn't the thing that made my mouth drop open. It was the fact that Zeus's statue was missing its head.

11

When I woke up the following morning it was almost 10am. Breakfast was over but a pot of coffee and some scones were waiting for me in the kitchen. I wasn't sure what I should do with myself, so I wandered through the house a bit. I found a ballroom that looked like it hadn't been used in ages, and then a library. I'd thought Able's office was impressive, but it was nothing like this.

Thousands of ancient leather books were stacked high and overflowing from shelves. Long oak tables divided the room, with antique green lamps evenly spaced between them. The ceiling was so high it looked like a cathedral, and it was painted with a fresco of the constellations that reminded me of the Sistine Chapel. Glass cases held antiques, and there were also a handful of large standing globes and statues. Like everything else in the house, it was luxurious, but somehow, all the books made me feel at home.

I wanted to just curl up on one of the leather couches and hide all day. I was dreading another sparring match. While my wounds seemed to be healing, they were still painful. But I wasn't here to read. Able had brought me here for a reason, and I had six days left to find out what that reason was—and whether or not I deserved to be here.

The first person I found was Sam, sitting in a cushioned bench by a large window. He looked up from a journal he was holding and smiled.

"Writing a book?" I teased, sitting next to him.

"Would you believe I've written dozens already? But no, I'm actually writing a poem."

"About what?"

"You," he said with a sly grin. "Unfortunately I don't know enough about you yet to finish it. But I will someday. Then I'll write a song for you."

"It's a deal," I said. A gust of wind sent a handful of orange and brown leaves sailing past the window.

"Do you know if I'm supposed to be anywhere? I mean, what do people normally do all day?"

"In the house? Whatever gives us pleasure. We all have our own interests. I'm sure you heard some of the excitement last night."

Was he referring to Tori and Dion? *Had he seen me?* My cheeks were turning red. This conversation had taken an awkward turn.

"Isn't pleasure kind of, I don't know, frivolous?" I asked.

His eyes grew round and somber. "We don't take pleasure for joy," he said, "we do it to distract ourselves."

"From what?" I asked.

"From the crippling emptiness of having our loved ones murdered; the perennial fear that we are prolonging the inevitable; the shame of knowing deep down, we don't care enough to stop it."

I bit my lip to keep my jaw from dropping, and wiped my palms on my jeans. This kid was way smarter than he looked. I'd have to be careful around him.

"You *are* a poet," I said finally.

He smiled and jumped down from the window.

"Let's go see Stephanie," he said. "If you really can see the future, we'd better learn to use it. A gifted seer makes a powerful ally… or a dangerous enemy."

Stephanie opened the door when Sam knocked. She was wearing a simple blue dress that accentuated her petite figure.

"Sorry about dinner last night," she said. She was wearing work gloves and filling a vase up with roses. "Please don't be too angry with Mist. She has had to deal with great tragedies."

"As have I," Sam said. "And Kaidance is no stranger to suffering. It shouldn't be an excuse for bad behavior."

I felt like hugging him. "It's fine. I understand," I said.

I stood there awkwardly for a few moments, before Stephanie finished her arrangement and looked me over. I was wearing dark jeans again, the black all stars, and a black tank top under a light jacket—plus of course the gloves Able had given me. Alice cleaned the blood off them, and they were good as new, apart from a tear from where the arrow had cut me. It was amazing how light they were—I could barely feel them.

"Sam, I think we should give Kaidance a break today. Why don't you play a game with her?" she leaned over and whispered in his ear. He smiled. Then he picked up a few tangerines that had been sitting in a silver dish on the table and started juggling them.

"Outside, please," Stephanie said, then she turned back to her flowers. Sam led the way downstairs and out a side door to a grassy patio on the side of the house.

"Catch!" he yelled as soon as we were outside. He tossed one of the tangerines over his shoulder. I caught it, but I didn't see the second one coming—he threw it like a baseball straight into my stomach. It didn't hurt much, but it took me by surprise. I wanted to yell at him but his playful look made me laugh instead. I threw the tangerines back at him, and he tossed me several more. It started out fun at first, but soon grew tiresome. My back ached, and I fumbled the oranges half the time. Soon I stank of citrus. Every few throws he would hit me square in the face, and make my black eye start pounding again.

I wondered what Sitri and Able were doing. Was this seriously the best use of my time? They brought me here but were too busy to teach me anything? Maybe Able had already given up on me and was just waiting for my time to run out so he could send me home. Even Stephanie's flowers were more important than me, apparently, so she'd passed me off to Sam as some kind of temporary babysitter.

After thirty minutes, Sam ran into the house to get a wine bottle, and told me to hold still as he balanced it on my head. I was supposed to catch the tangerines and throw them back without letting it fall.

"Some game," I muttered.

"It's not really a game," Sam said. "We're trying to help you."

"Seriously? How is this going to help?"

"Awareness. Discipline. Balance. Reflexes. Repetitive, focused action. It's better than meditation, and teaches you poise and balance at the same time. Everybody does it when they first come here. There's another game we play, where everybody has one orange, and we have to knock the bottles off other people's heads. Last one standing wins."

That made me feel a little better. Maybe this wasn't a waste of time. I pulled my hair back into a ponytail and decided to try harder.

"Well, I think I'm getting better at this," I said.

"No, you totally suck at it," he smirked. "Want to do something cooler?"

We walked out behind the house, past the ruins and up over the top of the theater. Surrounding the theater was a forest, and in the center was a wide dirt path, almost a road. There were two large sphinx statues on either side, marking some kind of entrance. Beyond the gate, we came to rows of...not tents exactly. They looked like a combination of a yurt and a log cabin. But bigger. As we kept walking, I saw that they extended in every direction. Hundreds of them.

There were even some built into the trees, suspended between branches. Groups of them were connected by long, hanging rope bridges. As we went deeper into the woods, there were more and more people. Kids mostly. Few of them could be older than twenty, though I was seriously doubting my age-meter here. In the middle of the woods was a little town, with a sprawling central garden, and what looked like Robin Hood's shopping mall. There were restaurants, coffee shops and stores. Some boys were playing Frisbee in a wide grassy area. It smelled like pine sap and burnt coffee grounds.

People kept stopping to look at us. I wondered if they were looking at me or Sam. One of the larger buildings looked like a ski lodge, with big glass panels in the front. Sam pushed the door open and I followed him inside. Sitri and Alice were sitting at a table, laughing about something.

"Thought you might be here," Sam said to Alice. For a fleeting second she looked guilty, as if he were chastising her. I wondered why. "Could you take out Kai's stitches?"

"Oh, sure!" she said. The building had high ceilings and a wide, comfortable living area. The interior was sleek and modern, which contrasted with the panorama forest view through the floor-to-ceiling windows. I watched Alice open cupboards to pull out equipment, and realized this was a hospital or health center of some kind.

"You've got all your tools here?" I asked, as she prepared a sterilization pad and a pair of surgical scissors.

"The other one is my home office. This is my day job," she said.

"There are other healers in town," Sam said. He was being weird. Something was definitely going on between him and Alice. Was she not supposed to be here?

"I'd go crazy if I couldn't help out. There's nothing to do at the house," Alice said. "And I don't care for the company."

"You can't choose your family," Sam said.

Alice led me into a smaller room that looked more like a traditional doctor's office. She had me sit on the narrow bed in the middle of the room and started removing the stitches in my ear.

"Aren't stitches supposed to stay in for a couple weeks?" I asked. "Does that mean I'm healing quickly?"

"Unfortunately, probably not," Alice said. "It's probably just an incidental side effect of staying at Nevah. There's a lot of energy here, the place is full of it. The house especially. It has a restorative effect on all of us."

I took off my gloves so Alice could work on my finger. She took the stitches out one by one with a pair of tweezers.

"Is everything okay between you and Sam?" I asked, as she cleaned the wound and added a fresh bandage.

"Caught that did you?" Alice said with a strained smile. "Some members of my family don't approve of me spending so much time down here."

"Why would they care?" I asked.

"Immortals and heirs aren't really that different. I mean we differ by degrees. We're all special according to the amount of energy in our bloods. The ones in the house have purer blood. They're a thousand times more powerful than anyone out here. A few of them feel superior, so they think they should remain separate. But some of the people in this camp are pretty old too, and they're fascinating. And they're a lot more fun to be around. Even though they're my family, it's lonely and isolating up there. Down here, there's life. There's love."

There was a funny look in her eye, and I wondered who she was talking about. Alice checked my bandages. I pulled my gloves back on, then we joined the boys in the main area.

"Sitri," Sam said, "Kai needs a new challenge. When's the last time you did the gauntlet?"

"Is that what you came here for?" Alice said, putting her hands on her hips. "I *just* took out her stitches!"

"She's here to learn," Sitri said, shrugging. "It's better than sitting around all day."

The four of us walked through the woods until we came to a tree with blocks of wood nailed to the trunk in a makeshift ladder. I looked up in awe at the sprawling ropes course above us. Sam climbed the ladder and jumped out onto a tightwire, with no safety wire or helmet. He didn't even stick his arms out, like they do in the movies. I wanted to yell at him to be careful, but it looked like he knew what he was doing.

"This one tests balance," he called.

He strolled down the wire casually, with his arms behind his back. He stopped, pretended to sniff a flower, then skipped to the next platform. My heart was pounding and I felt dizzy just watching him. Next there was a series of logs with large gaps between them, hanging like a wobbly bridge. Sam took these in long strides, sticking to the swinging pieces of wood like he had magnets under his feet.

"That one tests agility," he said when he'd reached the next platform safely. "But this one is my favorite. Heph whipped it up." Sitri hit a button on a panel at the base of a tree, and sections of the trees started spinning around. The trees were mechanized somehow—they looked like that part of a car wash with those spinning rags. But on a massive scale, with giant, old growth redwoods.

Sam dove headfirst between the swinging branches, swung himself off one and did a somersault in midair, before landing nimbly on a moving branch and launching himself off it like a trampoline. My mouth was hanging open by the time he landed on the next platform. I'd seriously underestimated Sam. I realized I'd been treating him like a kid. A little brother. He grabbed one of several metal hooks with a handle and a leather strap attached to it, and swung down on an angled wire.

"Your turn," he said with smirk, after landing in a roll and popping up just in front of us.

"Seriously?" I looked at Sitri and Alice. "There's no way I could do that."

"There are dozens of different paths through the course. People who attempt that last one usually break a few bones. Except ninja boy here," he said. "You can just do the easy ones."

"What if I fall?" I asked.

"Better to break your leg here, under our supervision, than in a real fight," Alice said.

"But I don't *want* to break my leg," I said, wishing I'd stayed in the library. "And I *hate* fighting."

Sitri put his hand on the small of my back and guided me towards the ladder. My arms were already shaking as I climbed the wooden blocks. I took a deep breath and stepped onto the wire, reaching my hands out on either side. I flailed back and forth, then tried to move my foot forward. I took two steps before slipping. I yelped as the ground rushed up at me. Something warm and hard broke my fall—*Sitri.*

"I can't believe you caught me," I said, breathless.

"I'd never let you fall," Sitri whispered. His blue eyes sparkled and I could feel his warm breath on my cheek.

The forest quickly fell into shadow as the sun went down. People lit lamps along the path and in front of the shops. The addition of glowing fireflies, which I'd never seen in the Northwest, made the setting magical, like a fairy village. I smelled meat cooking and realized I hadn't eaten all day. My stomach rumbled.

"I suppose that means it's dinner time," Sam said. "Let's go find Chandler."

We entered a wide clearing with multiple fire-pits. The sky was clear, and I could already see a scattering of stars in the deep purple tapestry.

People gathered around the fires, cooking in pots and pans.

"Do you eat every meal like this?" I asked. "Isn't it a lot of work?"

"What takes more effort," a voice boomed from behind me, "a billion dollar infrastructure, with tens of thousands of workers, to make a plastic spoon and then melt it down to make another one? Or washing your damn spoon?"

I turned around to see the speaker—he was older than most people I'd met at Nevah, maybe Able's age. He was holding a stick over his shoulder with half a dozen wild hares hanging from it. He stopped at one of the fire pits just ahead, and we filed in after him.

"That's Chandler," Alice whispered as we sat on one of the logs surrounding the fire. "He's kind of the unofficial leader out here." Chandler dressed the hares efficiently. Then he added the fresh hares to the homemade spit, while removing a few that were done cooking. He pulled chunks of meat off the bone and onto a large plate, which he offered to us. I took my gloves off so I wouldn't get them greasy.

"This is Matt and Curt," Sitri said, nodding at our nearest neighbors.

Matt had a nose ring and thin eyes that almost looked Asian—but I think they just looked like that because he was so beefy. He held a hand out to greet me. I held a gloved hand out towards his and shook. "I'm Kaidance."

Curt looked small sitting next to him, but actual he was about Sitri's size. He had long brown hair that he kept pushing out of his face as he was eating. His fingers were greasy from a piece of meat so he just nodded towards me with an apologetic shrug.

"So you're the new girl, hanging out with the royals?" said a girl with tightly braided hair, reaching down and grabbing a chunk of meat off Matt's plate, before sitting between Matt and Curt. She was wearing boots and some kind of leather bodice.

"I guess so," I said.

"You must be pretty special if they're keeping you in the house," Matt said.

"Special at getting my ass kicked," I said.

"She fought Mist her first day here. Slapped her in the face," Sitri said, grinning.

Matt whistled slowly, and I saw more than one set of raised eyebrows.

"Is that unusual?" I asked.

"I don't think anybody has laid a finger on Mist in a long, long time," Sam said.

"She must have been going easy on you," the girl said, digging into her food with her fingers. "I'm Priya, by the way."

"Sure," Sitri said, "if by 'easy' you mean shooting arrows at her, and then using her like a punching bag until she couldn't stand up."

"You know what I mean," Priya said. "In a real fight she would have just taken you out. Slashed one of your arteries. Or put an arrow through your heart from a mile away. I mean, you've seen her in battle, right? No offence Kaidance, but she can take out a hundred warriors by herself. I don't see how you could have offered her a real challenge."

I was about to argue, but what was I going to say—that I really was capable of fighting? I was the least qualified here. Priya was probably right, it must have been a lucky hit.

"So did they figure out your powers yet?" Matt asked.

"Only if clumsiness is a superpower," I said. If today was any indication of my skill level, I sucked.

"She lasted three seconds on the gauntlet," Sam said. "Tomorrow, it's back to oranges."

"You won't hear me complaining," I smiled. "Oranges sound about right."

"It always starts like that," Curt said. "They make you feel stupid, so you'll know how much further you need to come. Strip out your pride and self-confidence. Then they train you right."

"Train us, for what?" I asked.

"Hunters, remember?" Sitri said. "We're safe here, but in the real world, someone is always trying to kill us. We have to learn to protect ourselves."

"And each other," Alice said.

"Because you're different?" I asked.

"We are the truth that reveals his lie," Chandler said suddenly. I thought he was going to say more, or explain himself, but he just went back to stirring a pot of stew. He seemed to like talking in riddles. It was getting warm by the fire, so I took my jacket off, leaving just my black tank-top on. After I'd finished eating I wiped my hands and put my gloves back on.

"Don't worry," Curt said, "I'm sure they'll figure out your power soon. If not, you can move out here with the animals!"

Alice and Sam shifted uncomfortably.

"You know we don't call you that," Alice said.

"I've heard Mist say it," Sitri grunted.

"Wait, why would they call you animals?" I asked.

Matt looked at Sitri, who nodded at him.

"Okay man, but you owe me another shirt."

Matt set down his plate. Then his upper body stretched up and out like a balloon, until it had tripled in size. His hands became black hooves and a pair of sharp, curved horns grew from the sides of his head.

I stumbled backwards, as the beast put his nose inches from mine, and then grunted, snorting puffs of steam out of each nostril. The other kids laughed as Matt changed back, his shredded shirt now hanging off him in pieces. I picked myself up off the ground and wiped my hands. I tried to keep it cool as I took my seat, even though my heart was pounding.

"You're half bull?" I said weakly.

"Minotaur," Matt said. "I'm not really half anything. I'm a shifter. I can control what parts of me shift."

"Check this out," Curt said. As I watched, his ears grew long and pointy. Then his nose and jaw elongated until there was a horse's head on Curt's body.

"And don't ask me why the long face," Curt said, with his enormous teeth and round eyes. "You have no idea how many times I've heard that one."

"A centaur? Who are you guys related to?"

"Zeus, most likely," Alice said. "Pure bloods have so much energy, they can use it to transform their whole DNA. Zeus transformed into hundreds of different animals to seduce women."

"I never understood why he didn't just become human, if he wanted to sleep with a shepherd's daughters," Priya said. "It's like he had some kind of bestiality fetish."

"I think it was just a way to get past protective fathers," Alice said. "He'd turn into an animal first, a swan, a bull, a tiger, a butterfly even. Even when fathers locked their daughters up in towers, Zeus would find a way to get to them. But then word would get out, and he'd have to find a new disguise. Anyway, the child of such a union would be a shifter, and be able to take on the shape Zeus used in his seduction."

"So we're all bastards," Curt said.

"Some of us more than others," Matt said.

"We're not monsters," Curt said. "Although, we can be. If we want to make an impression, we can just half shift. It's usually impractical, but sometimes it can be cool."

"Is everyone out here a shifter?" I asked.

"No, but to pure-bloods, even heirs are animals," Priya said. "Present company excluded." She said this looking at Sam, and he nodded back to her.

"Not all pure-bloods are the same," Sitri said. "Remember, the ones at Nevah are *protecting* everybody here. Even if they consider heirs inferior, they still believe in their right to exist."

"Unlike Zeus and his side of the family," Heph said, coming up and joining the circle. He was carrying several large glass jugs and passed them out. Sitri greeted him with a pat on the back and several of the others shook his hand. He was popular out here.

"Mead," Sitri said, taking a sip straight from the jug and wiping his mouth with his sleeve. He passed me the jug and I took a sip. It was sweet, like honey.

"Zeus wanted to reform things," Heph said bitterly. "He started by murdering half of his family, and then tried to get rid of his unwanted children by killing off all the heirs. We fled Europe when the persecution began. We came here, a nearly virgin continent, where we lived in the open for thousands of years."

"That's how old this place is?" I asked. "Why doesn't anybody else know about it?" I asked.

"Able put up some charms and wards that keep it hidden to normal humans," Heph said. "And I added some more modern touches recently. There are few powerful enough to find it without being brought here."

"But, don't you have human parents?" I asked. "You're descendants, right? What are you, seventeen, eighteen?"

"If you mean eighteen hundred, you're only off by a few thousand years," Matt said.

I almost choked on my food. I grabbed the jug and gulped down some mead.

"Not everybody here is that old," Alice said. "Many of them are heirs—descendants. And Zeus didn't stop his antics a long time ago. Some of the ones here were born in the last few centuries, and have as much power as those sired thousands of years ago. And there are *also* some who were born by human parents, who got a bit of divine blood in their family tree centuries ago."

"Some of us are even older," Sitri said in a low voice that only I could hear. "Chandler was fathered by Cronus, before Zeus overthrew him. So he's actually Zeus's half-brother, but not as powerful, because he's half-human, whereas Zeus was born of Cronus and his sister Rhea—two Titans."

"Is he a shifter too?" I asked, looking at Cronus.

"He's the first satyr. Cronus took his mother in the form of a horse. Now you know where Zeus gets it," Sitri said. "Like father, like son."

My mind was starting to get confused from the mead. "How can everyone here be so old, but look so young?" I asked.

"Once our energy is activated, it keeps us looking young for a long time," Alice said. "We age slowly, if at all—especially if we have reserves to draw on."

"That's part of it," Sitri clenched his jaw. "The other reason most of the heirs at Nevah look so young is because they were too young to fight when the hunters found them and killed their parents. At a certain age, magical parents get found by Zeus's agents of death."

"Priya is your age," Matt said. "Human parents. She barely escaped by using some of her power."

"I never knew my parents were special," Priya said. "They hid it well. Then one day some men broke in. I knew something was off about them.

They had tattoos on their arms and glowing eyes. My mother pushed me into a closet. I watched them kill her, and covered my mouth to keep from screaming. Then they opened the closet. I couldn't understand why they couldn't see me. They looked right at me, then left anyway. I was on the street for a month before Sitri found me and brought me here."

She reached out and squeezed Matt's hand. Then she disappeared. My jaw dropped and several people laughed. I could just see Priya's eyes and teeth, they looked like they were floating.

"Invisibility?" I asked.

"Not completely," she said. "That's rare. More like very good camouflage. Like a chameleon."

"It's common for abilities to trigger during extreme stress—that's why Stephanie has been so rough on you," Alice said.

"Maybe," I said. "Though I think Mist just enjoys hurting me."

I heard music, and saw Sam holding an antique lyre that sparkled in the fireplace. He started to sing, and someone else joined him. I felt drawn to the music, so I went and sat next to him. The songs were from a different time, in languages I didn't recognize. Each was more beautiful than the last.

"I made this lyre for my older brother," Sam said during a pause in the music. "But he died before I could give it to him."

"I'm sorry," I said. "My brother died too."

"Did you try to save him?"

"Yes," I said. "With all my heart."

"I didn't," Sam said, with a sad smile. "I ran away and hid, to save myself."

"I'm sure there's nothing you could have done," I said. "You must have been really young."

"I was," he said. "Young and stupid. I won't hide next time." His fingers were clenched the instrument tightly. I put an arm around shoulders and gave him a quick squeeze.

Then I wrapped my fingers around my lego block necklace, thinking about my brother. Since the death of my brother, I've felt alone. Even after I had Jessie and Sarah, I longed for the holiday family dinners I remembered from my childhood. I had a sense of that at the house, but realized now how stiff and out of place I'd felt. Looking at the friendly faces around the campfire, my stomach full of meat and mead, I felt happier than I had in a long time. Even if everybody was suffering from their own personal tragedy—or perhaps because of it—I felt like I belonged.

The sky was totally dark now. The stars twinkled through patches of gray clouds, and sometimes we could see the crescent moon with a halo around it. I wondered what Sarah and Jessie were doing back at JDRI. It felt like a lifetime ago I'd been there with them.

"We're heading back," Alice said, interrupting my thoughts. Sam stood up to join her. "Kai, do you want to come with us?"

I wasn't eager to return to the house, as luxurious as it was. I wanted to savor the moment.

"Do I have to?" I asked.

"I can walk her back later," Sitri said. I glanced over at him. Was he staying because of me? After seeing him and Alice together earlier, I thought maybe they had a thing. I met his eyes and I felt my skin tingle, with the thought of us walking home together, alone. Did he like me—or was he just protecting me? Maybe that was his job.

"I'll go with you," Heph said, standing up. "Got to get back before the wife gets worried."

"Who are you married to?" I asked.

"Tori," he said. "Did I forget to mention that?"

My breath caught in my throat.

Heph and Tori are *married?* The image of what I'd seen through the keyhole flashed in front of my eyes. Did Heph know that Tori and Dion were sleeping together? Suddenly I felt claustrophobic. My palms were sweating and my chest felt tight. I needed some air. I pushed up and said something about going to the bathroom.

I didn't see Matt coming from the other direction until he was right in front of me. He grabbed me to keep me from running into him, his palms on my bare shoulders.

"What's the hurry," he said, grinning.

That's when I saw him die.

12

"That's insane," Mist snapped, "they would never attack us here."

"She saw what she saw," Sitri said gruffly, crossing his arms. Able held up his hand for silence. We were in the main dining hall, but the table was clear—the wood was so polished I could see a reflection of the tense faces around it.

After running into Matt I'd grabbed my coat and pulled Sitri away from the fire to tell him what I'd seen. We came back to the house and told Able. He called this meeting. The others had just arrived.

"Why don't you go through it one more time," Able said. "Even the smallest detail could be important."

I squeezed my eyes shut, trying to remember.

Pieces of the vision came back to me. Matt lying in a pool of blood. The blood soaking into the ground. Something shiny. Flashes of smoke and fire.

"It was dark," I said. "I couldn't see the attacker."

"What about the ground beneath him?" Sam asked.

"Dirt," I said. "And grass."

"How soon will it happen?" Heph asked.

"I don't know. Usually within a few months."

"She's worthless," Mist said. "What are we supposed to do with that?"

"What about the weapon?" Sitri prompted.

I concentrated on the image in my mind. Blood. Darkness. Something shiny—*a sword.*

"It was sticking up out of his chest," I said, touching the place over my heart. "A gleaming sword. The handle was set in gold, with blue stones. And there was a symbol… a crown I think."

"The royal emblem," Stephanie said solemnly. "All the hunters carry a sword like that. They think they're protecting their one true king. There is no way she could have known that."

"She could have seen it when we were attacked earlier," Sitri said. "Even if she didn't register it consciously."

"Maybe Matt was planning on leaving the property," Tori said. "He could have been attacked somewhere else. Outside of Nevah."

"So we just make sure he sticks around. That's easy enough," Dion said.

Able sat in the chair at the head of the table and leaned back thoughtfully. The jeweled rings on his fingers sparkled as he stroked his beard. One of them stood out—a blue sapphire so dark it was nearly black, with a star-shaped asterism that slid along the surface of the gem as he moved. The golden ring was engraved with symbols I didn't recognize.

"Nobody has ever attacked Nevah directly," he said. "But that doesn't mean they never will. It's inevitable that Zeus would want to finish this war."

"I didn't see a war," I said. "I just saw Matt."

"But Matt's also the only one you touched, right?" Sitri said.

I nodded.

"So we have her do her thing with everybody," Heph said. "Gather as much information as possible. Maybe she'll see something that will tell us when the attack is coming."

I nodded, even though I was dreading it. Seeing just one death was a terrifying experience for me. I'd always tried to *avoid* it.

"I think we'll have to assume," Able said, "that we are no longer completely safe at Nevah. Zeus has left us alone in the past, because he knows another all-out battle could shift things in our favor. Instead he's been picking us off, one by one, whenever he could catch one of us alone."

"But why now? What's changed?" Dion asked.

"They want Kaidance," Sitri said. "She's important for some reason."

"Important enough to start a war? To challenge us here?" Heph asked, looking me over doubtfully.

"If they're after her, why don't we just give her up? Or better yet, finish her off ourselves?" Mist flung me against the wall and lifted me up with one hand, her fingers digging into my throat. Her other hand pulled a dagger out of a sheath on her thigh. *She's going to kill me.* Suddenly my vision became sharper, the lights in the room brighter. As adrenaline surged through my body, things slowed down, like they had earlier with the arrow. I could see Sitri jumping over a chair to grab Mist's arm, and Able yelling at her to stop. Tori remained at the table looking on with mild interest. Dion reached for his wine glass.

Then I saw the thread again. More clearly this time. The whole world blurred, and this single golden thread, floating gently before me, was all I could see. As it came into focus, it gave off a high pitched whine. It was singing—calling to me. I reached out with my gloved fingers, and it grew straight and firm as I neared. I plucked it like a guitar string and released it with a *twang*. Mist's eyes rolled back in her head. She dropped the knife and fell to the floor like a ragdoll.

There was a second when time seemed to freeze altogether, as everyone in the room paused to look at me with disbelief. Then life jolted back to regular speed. Stephanie screamed and charged at me. Able restrained her in his powerful arms.

Heph and Alice picked Mist up off the floor. Her face was as pale as death, and she looked at me with a mixture of awe and terror.

"Well, that was unexpected," Dion said, sipping his wine.

"What *are* you?" Mist asked, her voice trembling. I couldn't think of a response.

"Get her out of here," Able yelled. "Take her to my study."

Sitri grabbed my hand and pulled me out the door. He wouldn't even look at me, he just sat me down in Able's office and left me there to wait in silence. I felt sick. The pleasant feelings from earlier had vanished. I'd gotten too comfortable. I'd started to believe that maybe I wasn't a curse, a monster. Maybe I was a victim, like everyone else here. Now I knew the truth. I could see it in the way they'd looked at me, as Mist crumpled to the ground. The horror on their faces. After what felt like a really long wait, Able and Sitri came back in.

"Is she okay?" I asked.

"She'll be fine," Able said.

The knot in my stomach loosened slightly. I took a deep breath as Able sat on the couch across from me and fixed me with his dark eyes.

"Have you ever done that before?" he asked.

"I don't even know what I did," I said.

"Tell me exactly what happened." I explained how things slowed down, and I saw the string and touched it. Able didn't look surprised.

"Have you ever seen a thread like that before?"

"Just once, after Mist beat the crap out of me."

"Did you know it would hurt her?"

I shook my head.

"My wife wants me to kill you," Able said, frowning.

"That's ridiculous!" Sitri said. "She didn't do it on purpose."

"She's dangerous," Able said. "That much is obvious. But to hurt Mist… heirs shouldn't have the power to hurt immortals. I mean other than ganging up on one, holding them down and cutting off their heads or something. That rarely happens because they can't be contained. Mist could fight a hundred heirs without breaking a sweat. I've seen her slaughter thousands of men. To think that an untrained girl like you—"

"But how?" Sitri asked. "You must have some idea."

Able nodded. "I didn't believe it at first, even after I saw her wrist."

"I don't see how that's related," I said.

"Then allow me to educate." Able opened a cabinet and took out a bottle of brandy and several crystal glasses. "Let me start with the stuff you probably learned in school." He handed me a glass. My hands were trembling when I took it.

"I didn't exactly get a formal education," I said, taking a sip of the alcohol. It burned my throat and warmed my stomach.

"But you've heard of the Olympians."

"Like what, the winter games?" I knew what he was getting at but I didn't want to make it easy for him.

"The gods and goddesses of Olympus," he said.

"Mythology, right?"

"You should know better by now. After all, you've met some of them."

"You mean their descendants."

He gave me a grim smile. Wait, was he saying that some of the gods of Olympus were actually at Nevah? Able went to the bookshelf, opened his secret door, and returned holding a horned goat skull. He set it down on the table and handed me a magnifying glass.

"Let's start from the beginning. You can follow along with this visual history," he said, pointing to the place on the skull that began the narrative.

"Once upon a time, as you like to say, the world was ruled by the Titans. Chief among them was Cronus and his sister Rhea. Cronus heard a prophecy that one of his children would overrule him, so he ate them all, one after the other. Until Zeus. Zeus escaped, and he *did* overthrow his father and save his brothers and sisters, rescuing them from Cronus' stomach. Zeus killed his father, divided up the universe with his two brothers, and for a time, there was peace."

Able swirled his brandy in its glass. I waited for him to continue. His brows furrowed, as if he were reminiscing, rather than recounting children's tales.

"But then Zeus got greedy. He didn't like sharing power. He wanted to be the sole ruler. So he decided to kill his brothers, and all of his sons and daughters, and wipe out magic from the world, leaving his reign undisputed and unchallenged. He became paranoid, accusing everyone of plotting a revolution to challenge his rule. He started creating soldiers. He said it was for the protection of Mount Olympus, and all of the immortals, but they were really his own personal army."

"Meanwhile, no one was looking out for the race of men. The gods of Olympus used them like chess pieces, waging war against each other, for fun and spite. Zeus used the human race like his own personal harem. Zeus's brother Poseidon, and his son Apollo were fond of humans, and they hatched a plan to overthrow him—but Zeus got wind of it. So he invited everyone to dinner, and he poisoned Poseidon. Then he killed Apollo, his favorite son. He hacked him into pieces on the dining table. At the same time, he had his daughter, Athena, assassinate Ares, the strongest of his sons. She asked to speak to him privately, then stabbed him in the back with a poisonous dagger."

I was trying to keep track of the story but my brain was getting fuzzy. I'd heard these names before and tried placing them. Poseidon, god of the ocean. Ares, god of war. Apollo, god of the sun.

"Athena… goddess of wisdom? Why would she kill Ares?"

"Mostly, because her daddy told her to. But also because Ares and Athena hated each other. Ares believed in brute strength. Honest combat. Athena loved military strategy—deception and manipulation. Ares was stronger, but Athena was more devious. Challenged to a fair duel, Ares would have won, no question. But he underestimated her. She proposed a truce and then stabbed him when his guard was down. Honor wouldn't have let him do what she did."

"Zeus commanded his newly made army to kill everyone else. There was a great battle, but Zeus's forces were greater, and the surviving Olympians went into hiding. Only his wife Hera, and his daughter Athena, stayed with him. They were the only two he trusted."

We'd reached the other side of the skull, and I could see the three figures standing alone on Mount Olympus, over a pile of bodies.

"I still don't understand what any of this has to do with me," I said.

"When Zeus's surprise attack failed, and most of the Olympians went into hiding, he tried to use the *Moirai*—the Fates—to finish them off."

Able turned the skull over and I could see the carvings continued on the other side. A large carving of three women was in the middle, followed by miniscule scenes around the edges. I marveled at the detail, running my fingers over the smooth bone.

"Clotho spins the thread of life; Lachesis determines how long one lives by measuring it; and Atropos chooses how someone dies by cutting the thread of life with her shears. Some say they were Zeus's own daughters, but they were actually born of the Titan Themis."

"They'd always been left to their own devices, but when Zeus took over, he started controlling their powers. He would tell them who to kill, who to give tragedy or wealth, health or sickness. The Fates used to be mostly random, accidental and mysterious. Under Zeus, those loyal to him were rewarded, and those who weren't, punished."

I shared a look with Sitri, who was standing in the corner with his arms crossed. He looked as anxious and frustrated as I felt. Why were we getting a history lesson right now, when there were more important things to talk about?

"After the failed rebellion, the remaining heirs and immortals took refuge here, in Nevah, where Zeus's armies couldn't reach them. So he commanded the Fates to start killing the immortals. Only they have the power to sever a divine thread, and it usually takes all three of them together. But the Fates ran, and hid the golden shears. Without their powers, Zeus had to stop his slaughter."

"He regrouped and started a massive propaganda campaign against the other gods and their progeny, convincing the world that they were merely myth and folklore. At best, childish stories. At worst, witchcraft and devilry. Since then, he's used his hunters to finish us off quietly. The rest of us are still alive, only because of the Fates' refusal of Zeus's command. They are our saviors, our religion, our mothers. We exist in their resistance."

"I don't understand why we're talking about this," Sitri said, running a hand through his dark hair. "Nobody has seen the Fates in thousands of years. What do they have to do with Kaidance?"

Able reached for my arm, and gently pulled the glove off my left hand. He turned my wrist slowly, examining the red mark around my wrist. "I've heard rumors of a mark like this. The scarlet thread. It's very rare. It's said to be a gift from the Fates. That you've been chosen to receive their powers."

"That's impossible," Sitri said. "The Fates are virgins. They have no descendants."

"As far as we know," Able said. "Yet here she is. She may not be a descendent at all. Maybe the Fates chose her for some other reason. If you can see the threads of fate, then you may have received more of their powers. Like the power to sever the strings of life. That would make you an unstoppable weapon—and the world's most deadly assassin. If Zeus suspects you have that ability, he will do absolutely anything to kill you, before you destroy him."

13

I lay in bed late the next morning, hating myself as I looked around my luxurious bedroom. My stomach twisted with guilt when I thought about what I'd done to Mist. They'd brought me here as a guest, to *protect* me. Although I hadn't done it on purpose—and I was pissed off at Able for not sharing his suspicions earlier—a sick part of me was proud that I'd finally wiped the smug look off her face. I was tempted to say she deserved it, for bullying me all week. That's the part of myself I hated. Mist's face when I touched the thread haunted me. I've never seen anyone look so utterly defeated, so hopeless, so terrified. Like a lifetime of nightmares coming to life at the same time. I wanted to shrug it off, but I couldn't. I felt changed.

Since my brother died, people have looked at me a certain way. Like I was dangerous. Like I couldn't be trusted, because I might snap and accidentally kill someone. I'd been able to bear it because I knew it wasn't true. Until now. Suddenly, all those years, all those looks were justified. I *was* dangerous. And not just to myself.

I pulled the blankets over my face as the sun crept into the room. I was in no hurry to expose myself to the rest of the family. I wasn't prepared to handle the looks. The same looks I'd always faced, but this time, it wasn't just suspicion. This time their fears were justified. I was a monster.

I stayed in bed until I heard movement around the house. I couldn't pretend it was still too early to get up, and I knew Able and the others would be waiting for me. We'd tabled the discussion last night, when my I couldn't keep my eyelids open, but there was more I needed to find out. Like what we were going to do about Matt.

I took a shower, then went through my wardrobe. The stacks of brand new clothes made me feel worse about myself. I didn't deserve them; their sheen and softness was a reproach rather than a comfort.

I pulled on a pair of blue jeans and thick black sweater. Then I put on Charlie's necklace. I pushed it into my skin until the sharp points of the lego bricks dug into my collarbone. The pain made me feel better.

Sitri was waiting for me outside my door, snoozing on a chair he'd carried into the hall. I admired his rugged profile, the early morning light framing him in a soft glow, the dark stubble on his chin. He was wearing jeans and a pair of black boots, with a white tank top. He'd removed his other shirt and was using it like a pillow. I kicked one of his feet to wake him. He jumped up, instantly alert. One of his fists was pulled halfway back, as he searched frantically for a target. His eyes softened when he saw me. Then he shrugged sheepishly and let his arm fall.

"Did you sleep here?" I asked.

"Not really," he said. "I was having trouble sleeping. Every tiny noise got me out of bed to investigate, so finally I just thought it'd be easier to stay here."

"It's sweet of you to be so worried," I said. "But your room is literally right next to mine. Isn't that enough?"

"Through two closed doors? No way. They could come in and take you out the window, or the front door, and I'd never even know."

"Just because I had a vision doesn't mean it's going to happen soon. It could be a long time. Are you going to sleep in the hall for the next month?"

"If I have to." He flashed a determined smile. "Unless you want to keep the doors between us open."

I bit my lip. That would almost be like sharing a room. But I didn't want him sleeping in a chair. He deserved his rest.

"Okay," I said finally. "Open door policy. Except when I'm changing or in the bathroom."

Mist and Stephanie were eating breakfast when we walked into the dining room. Mist flinched when she saw me. The tension in the room was unbearable as I put some toast and eggs on my plate. Stephanie eyed us coolly as we sat down. It was impossible to relax under her gaze. For some reason her disapproving look was even more powerful on her young face.

"I'm so sorry about yesterday," I said, my voice breaking. "I never meant to hurt you."

Mist scoffed and rolled her eyes.

"You didn't hurt me," she said. "You just surprised me. Something that hasn't happened for a very, very long time. It's my fault. I let my guard down and underestimated you. I won't make that mistake again." She grabbed her plate and left the room, slamming the door behind her.

There was a long pause after she left, then Stephanie stood to leave as well. "I believe you didn't do it on purpose, because you would be incapable of lying to my husband or I. But if you ever harm Mist or anyone in this family again, I'll kill you."

I gulped as she left the room.

"It wasn't your fault," Sitri said quietly. "You didn't know what you were doing."

"Part of me wanted to hurt her," I admitted, stirring the scrambled eggs on my plate. "When she came at me, I was looking for weaknesses. I was looking for a way to do damage."

"But you didn't know what would happen. What *could* happen. Able shouldn't have kept that a secret. He should have told us. Or you at least."

After breakfast we went straight to Able's study. We knocked before entering. I felt a touch of excitement. After all, the conflict between Mist and I wasn't the only thing that happened yesterday. I'd seen Matt's death. And for the first time, people here *believed me*. I'd been waiting for a moment like this my whole life. To actually be able to warn someone in time to stop their death. If my attack on Mist made me feel guilty, maybe saving Matt would redeem me. Otherwise, what good were my powers, except for making me feel responsible for everyone I didn't warn?

"Come in," Able called. We entered the room to find Able in a pair of silk pajamas, leaning over one of his skulls with a pair of spectacles and tiny knife. It was something new, it looked like a miniature deer skull. The crystal decanter from the night before was empty, and there was an ash tray with a few cigar stubs. One was still burning. I wondered if Able had slept.

"What do you want us to do first?" Sitri asked.

Able ignored him, making a microscopic incision into the skull and then brushing away bits of bone with his fingertips.

"Do you want us to go warn Matt?" I asked hopefully.

"No." Able said, without looking up from his sculpture.

I was stunned by his answer. *No?*

"We put everyone on high alert. We tell them there is a threat of an attack. We bolster our defenses. But we don't tell Matt what you saw."

"He has a right to know," Sitri said.

"My decision is final," Able said calmly, returning to his work.

"But we have to save him!" I said. "Isn't that the whole point? To avoid death? He should hide."

"You think that's what he'd want?" Able said, looking up at me. His dark eyes were like thunderstorms. "If there's one thing I've learned in all my years, it's this: death will not be cheated. If he was meant to die, but doesn't, someone else will take his place. How would he feel if people die while he's hiding to protect himself?"

"If it were me," Sitri said, "I'd want to fight. You couldn't keep me from fighting. But I'd still want to know."

"And in knowing, what if your confidence was compromised?" I jumped when Stephanie started talking. She was standing in the corner behind us, but I hadn't seen her come in. Was she in the room before we got there?

"What if you hesitated, and it caused your death? A self-fulfilling prophecy?"

Sitri bit his lip for a moment, then nodded.

"We don't tell Matt," he agreed.

I couldn't believe this was happening. They believed me but they still weren't going to warn him? I looked between them, my mouth open.

"You can't just let him die," I said, gesturing vaguely with my hands.

"I'm not abandoning him. I'm suggesting that telling him isn't the best way to protect him. We'll bring him into the house. You said you saw him outside, so maybe that will help. But I can't worry about one person exclusively. I have a responsibility to everyone under my care. And of course, let's not forget: they probably aren't coming here for Matt. They're coming here for *you.*"

My throat felt dry and scratchy. I had no response to that.

"And more importantly, while Matt's death would be tragic, yours could be significantly worse. We still don't know exactly what they hope to do with you, whether they actually want to kill you or use you somehow. But if Zeus is after you, and willing to restart a war that has been cooling for several thousand years, the stakes are high. Maybe higher than we can imagine. So if anyone needs our attention it's you."

Sitri nodded grimly, rubbing his jaw.

"What do you want me to do?" I asked.

"I suggest a trip to the armory. Then, until they come for you, practice."

"Wait, you want her to fight?" Sitri asked. "You just said they're coming for her. She needs to be hidden. Guarded."

I wanted to disagree. I wanted to say something foolish like I could take care of myself. But seriously, after getting my ass kicked by Mist, I wasn't sure how well I'd fair in a real fight.

"Of course we'll protect her," Stephanie said. "And chances are, she'll never be in any real danger. But would you have her completely defenseless? Without even a weapon on her for emergencies? No, she should be armed. As for fighting, wouldn't you rather she learn what she can? What's the alternative, sitting around on her thumbs, like a princess, waiting for a knight to fight her battles for her?"

"I'm not a princess," I said, clenching my fists. Stephanie was right. Maybe I sucked at fighting, but that didn't mean I shouldn't try to get better. Plus, after what I'd done to Mist, it's not like I was completely defenseless. I'm not sure I wanted to do anything like that again—to inflict that kind of suffering on someone. On the other hand, it was better than running them through with a sword, right? Maybe I just needed to learn how to control it better.

I met Stephanie's eyes and nodded, to show my commitment. I needed to be able to defend myself. If I didn't, I put other people's lives at risk.

"The armory it is then," Stephanie said. "After that, come see me in my room."

The armory was a vast cellar with curving stone walls. The ceiling was raised like a cathedral, and large tapestries told the story of a hundred battles. On either end were statues so large that the entrance and exit to the room passed through their legs. Their shoulders were pressed into the ceiling like they were holding it up.

"Ares at one end, Athena at the other," Sitri said, pointing at the statues. "To remind soldiers it takes both strength *and* strategy to win a war."

Glass cases lined the walls, filled with all kind of weaponry. Hundreds of spears, swords, daggers and shields gleamed from display shelves. Some of the swords were so beautiful and finely made, they seemed to be glowing.

"This just seems so... *historic*," I said. "Can't we use something more modern? Like that gun you used last time?"

Sitri opened up one of the cases and pulled out a pair of twin swords with curved blades.

"Bullets won't stop hunters," he said. "They'll slow them down a lot, but you could fill them with bullets and they'd still reach you. And then they'd cut you in half. A sword is the only way to actually block their attack. Iron has been used as a defense against the supernatural for thousands of years. It basically diffuses energy, making it impossible to focus. All the hunters have swords that are charged with Zeus's nearly unlimited supply of energy. Iron takes away the obvious advantage one person would have, and makes the match a little more even, based on natural skill and strength."

"For me, a sword is best, so I can block and have a chance at attacking. For you, I'm not exactly sure yet. You haven't learned how to use any weapons. We could hide you behind a shield, but a powerful blow would crush you anyway."

Sitri pressed a concealed button on the stone wall and I gasped as the display case rotated, revealing a small room filled with modern guns and weaponry. It looked like something from a

James Bond film—we watched them sometimes when I was younger—the part where Q hands out spy gadgets.

Sitri picked up a sawed-off shotgun from the shelf and handed it to me. My hand sunk under the weight. Then he grabbed a handful of shells and slipped them into my pockets.

"Start with that," he said. "Point and shoot. The shells are filled with iron ball bearings. Like I said, it won't kill them, but it'll hurt, and reduce their ability to draw on Zeus's energy. It'll slow them down and make them weaker. At least then you'll have a chance."

"Should I have a sword too?" I asked.

"Pick one out," he said.

I ran my hand over a dozen of the swords mounted against the wall. The first I tried to pick up was so heavy I dropped it, and it clattered to the floor of the display case. Sitri hefted it back up for me.

"Maybe let's start off with something a little smaller," he said with a smirk. I reached for another. It felt lighter in my hands. Sitri nodded to the corner where three large practice mats were set up. They had a soft, spongy texture.

"Hold it up. Defend yourself," he said.

I raised the sword out in front of me and waited. He didn't attack. He just stood there, smiling at me. After less than a minute, my arm was shaking from the weight.

"I get the point," I said, lowering the sword. "Asshole."

"I'm not saying you can't learn to use it. But with no training, you need weapons you can use immediately. Right?"

I hated feeling like such a wimp, but I nodded.

Sitri walked down several cases and pulled out another sword. It was straight and razor thin, and less than an inch wide. He held it out to me carefully.

"Watch it with that," Heph said. "Made in Damascus—sharp enough to slice a falling piece of silk in half, strong enough to split stones without dulling. Craftsmen added wood and organic debris to their furnaces to release carbon. The carbon fused with the molten iron to produce carbon-laced steel, hard but flexible."

The light blade swung easily in my hand.

"So this is where the party is," said Sam, entering through the same door we had, under the legs of Athena. I paled as I saw him open one of the cases and pull out a weapon.

"You're not going to fight, are you?" I asked.

"I may be small, but I'm actually pretty good at this thing," he said, swinging the sword. It let out a metallic whine as it carved through the air.

"But it's dangerous," I said. *And you're just a kid.*

"I'll tell you what," he said, putting down the weapon and picking up a couple of wooden practice swords from a bin nearby, "we'll have a little match. If you can hit me, I won't fight."

"That's not fair," I said. "I've never even picked up a sword before. You won't be fighting me, you'll be fighting hunters."

"Sitri then. How about it, Sitri. Think you can land a blow? First to three wins?"

"I could use the practice," Sitri said.

Heph and I stood together, watching Sitri and Sam face off with the practice swords. Sam was about half the size of his opponent. He stood casually, in jeans and tennis shoes, looking like a freshman on his first day of high school. Sitri, in contrast, looked like an ex-convict. His muscles bulged under his white tank top, and his cropped dark hair made him look dangerous. He yelled and charged forward. Sam blocked the first swing, then vanished. He reappeared directly behind Sitri and took a casual swipe at his back.

"That's one," he said with a smirk.

My jaw dropped open. "How is he doing that?" I asked, gripping Heph's arm.

"Sam's the fastest creature I've ever known," Heph said. "And he's got a pair of shoes that make him even faster. He moves so quickly, it's like teleportation."

Sitri attacked again with a flurry of blows. Sam deflected each one gracefully. He didn't take the full weight of the blow with a direct block, he just held his sword in way that made Sitri's sword glance of it in a new direction. Sitri was fast, and relentless, but no matter what he tried, Sam blocked it.

Sitri lunged forward suddenly. Sam dropped to the ground and rolled under his attack. As Sitri tripped over him, Sam kicked him from behind and sent him sprawling. I laughed as Sam, still on the ground, stretched and stifled a yawn. Sitri jumped to his feet and took a wide swing—but Sam appeared behind him again with his sword to his throat.

"That's two," he said. I was beginning to appreciate Sam's confidence. He was untouchable.

"That's the problem with magic," Sitri said, breathing heavily. Sweat dripped down the side of his face. "You can never judge an opponent based solely on appearance. They may have magical abilities, or special objects that allow them to do unexpected things. If this was a real fight, you'd want to shoot him with the shotgun, or wrap him in iron netting. That might slow him down enough to get a blade in him."

"If this was a real fight," Sam said, "I'd have taken your head off and been on my tenth kill by now."

Sitri reached for another practice sword, so that he had one in each hand. "Do you mind?" he asked.

"Not at all," Sam said, with a little bow. Sitri growled as the strikes began to flow—he alternated both swords in a constant attack. Sam deflected them as before, but it was harder for him to keep up and block both at once with only one sword. Sitri lunged, swinging the swords together like a giant pair of scissors. There was no way Sam could block it. But when the swords came together and crossed in the middle, Sam was no longer between them. He was standing on one foot on top of Sitri's swords, like some kind of strange bird. He tapped Sitri lightly on the head, then did a backflip off the swords and landed gracefully.

"That's three," he said. "I win."

"I don't think you need any more practice," Sitri said.

"Heph, why don't you and Kai go sharpen these swords?" Sam reclaimed the weapon he'd chosen and tossed it to Heph. "Then we'll take them outside for some real practice."

I followed Heph through the back end of the armory, through the legs of Ares, into a room that looked like a medieval blacksmith forge. There was a side exit through the forge, and I could see grass outside. Heph sprinkled some water on a long sharpening stone and begin grinding one of the swords against it with long, practiced strokes. Even with the side door open, I was soon sweating from the heat of the forge. The orange glow lit up one side of Heph's face.

Being alone with Heph made me think about why I left the campfire—how this all got started. I felt like I was betraying him, by not telling him about Dion and Tori. But I didn't want to be a tattletale either, and it wasn't really my business. I just got here, and I didn't want to make any enemies.

"What's wrong?" Heph asked, without taking his eyes off the sword. His long dark hair fell around his face like a curtain.

"It's nothing. I was just thinking. How long have you and Tori been together? Married I mean?"

"A long, long time. It feels like forever sometimes," he said.

"But you're happy together?"

"We mostly live our own lives. We have very different interests. But I'm happy, and I think she's happy."

"You love her?" I asked.

"Yes," he said. There was a touch of fervency in his eyes. Devotion. That made it all the worse. My heart ached for him, he seemed like such a nice guy.

"I was actually supposed to marry somebody else. It was an arranged marriage. But the girl rejected me. Then my parents disowned me for disgracing them. Able is my uncle, he took me in, but I still wasn't allowed to come home, because I'd shamed my family." His brow furrowed, and he slid the sword so quickly against the stone that sparks flew.

"That's awful," I said.

"Tori changed all that. I met her when I was young, and we've always been friends. Tori could have had *anyone*—and she knows it. But she chose me. I think in part to slight my parents, and the girl who refused me. To make a point. Marrying Tori brought me home, back into the family. My parents couldn't say anything."

"Why did the first girl refuse you?" I asked.

"Because I'm disabled."

I gave him a look of disbelief. His bronze skin shone with sweat from working near the hot forge. He had a few scars, but mostly, like everyone else at Nevah, he looked strong, young and handsome. A model for perfection.

He grinned at me and took off one of his shoes. It took me a minute to even realize his left foot only had four toes.

"What, *that's it?* She rejected you because of that? What an idiot!"

"It might not seem so bad to you, but in my family, perfection is kind of a big deal."

Heph found me a scabbard and a wide leather belt, which he strapped around my waist. I heard voices, and stiffened when I saw Matt and Priya coming in through the forge's side entrance.

"Rumor at camp is we might be seeing some action," Matt said to Heph. "I thought I'd come give you a hand."

"I could use it," Heph said. "Most of the weapons will hold an edge for decades, but it's probably been a century since we've gone through the whole collection." As we headed back into the armory, Priya grabbed my arm.

"Do you know what's going on?" she asked. My skin prickled, and I was glad I was already sweating from being in the hot space.

"Why would I know? I just got here."

"Um, exactly. Nobody understands why hunters would attack us here. They've never done it before. There hasn't been a real battle since Zeus's first coup. We've had skirmishes, when we go out to find new survivors and try to bring them in. But if they're attacking here, there must be something they want. Or someone."

She raised an eyebrow at me. I felt like she was accusing me of something. And she was right, of course, but I couldn't let her know that.

"Plus you've been living in the house. You might hear things," Matt said, turning back. I didn't realize he'd been listening in.

"Able found a weapon," Sitri interrupted, taking over the conversation. I let out a breath of relief. "Something powerful. We're not sure how to use it yet, but we think Zeus is desperate to get it. We've already sighted scouts on the borders of the property. That's why we're preparing. Maybe it won't come to anything, but we should be ready. We want to bring in everybody from the camp and keep them closer to the house so we're less divided. And we'll put a defensive row of torches around that. That'll make it less likely a small group of hunters will be able to sneak in."

Matt nodded. I flinched as the image of him lying in a pool of blood, a sword through his heart, flashed in front of my eyes. Priya was looking at me but I looked away—I couldn't meet her eyes. I bit my lip and glared at Sitri.

"Matt, I'd like you to stay down here," Sitri said.

"In the armory?" Matt asked, confused. "But I should be upstairs, guarding the house. Fighting."

"You're more likely to see action down here," Sitri said. "If they're looking for a weapon, this is one of the first places they'll check."

"Is it down here?" Priya asked, reaching for Matt's hand. I watched them curl their fingers together, and my chest tightened uncomfortably.

"No," Sitri said. "But they don't know that. There's a good chance they'll come here first, before checking out other parts of the house. If they do, you can sound the alarm and keep them busy. We'll keep them contained in here, block the exits. Make sure they can't do any more harm."

"I'll stay with him," Priya said. "We'll take shifts." She stood against the wall and disappeared, using her camouflage trick to vanish against the stones. Then she reappeared and gave a thumbs-up.

"Let's go outside and teach you how to use that thing," said Sitri, pointing at the sword hanging from my hip. He found a leather satchel for the shotgun and some more shells, and slung that over my shoulder.

"Can we start with how I'm supposed to walk with all this stuff on?" I asked.

"You'll get used to it," Sam said.

We took the exit through the back of the forge and walked around the outside of the house. I could already see people moving in from the camp, setting up tents and building campfires. News spread quickly. The weather was cooler; it looked like it might rain. I took a deep breath of the clean, fall air, trying to get the image of Matt and Priya holding hands out of my mind. I felt terrible for not telling them about my vision. I let the scent of earth and pine needles sooth me.

"Feel better now?" Sitri asked.

"No," I said. "But Able was right. It's better if he doesn't know. Do you really think they'll come to the armory first?"

"No. But he'll be safe there. If the hunters are looking for you, they'll probably check upstairs first."

I felt a flicker of hope, followed by a sudden panic. When my brother died, I thought I hadn't tried hard enough to save him. I hadn't made myself clear. I hadn't convinced my parents to believe me. This time, people believed me. Maybe my abilities weren't a curse. Maybe I wasn't like Cassandra, doomed to be ignored. If people took my warnings seriously, and listened to me, maybe I could save them. But what about me?

Now that Matt was safe, the full scope of the situation hit me. We were preparing for an attack, because of a vision I saw. If I was right, and the hunters were coming, they were coming *for me*. I remembered the determined look on Puriel's face as he chased after us on his bike. Was he really trying to kill me? Would he kill others to get to me?

I froze as I saw a figure through the crowd ahead. He was tall and blond, and had something on his wrists that looked like tattoos. I clenched the handle of my sword, my arm trembling, as we locked eyes.

14

"It's okay," Sitri said, putting his palm on my shoulder. "He's a torch. Sorry, I should have prepared you better for that. They're on our side. You'll see more—they'll be on the perimeter."

I could see now that the man wasn't Puriel, though he could have passed for his brother. His tattoos were covered by scars that looked like they'd been seared into his flesh.

"What are they?" I asked, trying to keep my voice level. "Where do they come from?"

"They used to be hunters. Part of Zeus's private army. When Zeus ordered them to kill his own family, the immortals and other supernatural beings, some refused."

"Actually, that's not right," Sam said. "They didn't even get a chance to refuse. That would take a deliberate, conscious choice. All they had to do was hesitate. If they don't immediately obey every command from Zeus, without question, they get cast off. It's like a self-destruct mechanism built into Zeus's army. They ignite, and separate from his power."

"Why call them torches?" I asked.

"When they first fell," Sitri said, "there were thousands of them, falling like shooting stars, burning through the night sky. It looked like the sky was burning, and the whole world was filled with their screams. It was... a singularly unforgettable experience. Able gave them refuge. They mostly live in caves underneath Nevah."

"But they're on our side now?" I asked.

"Basically. Or at least, they aren't against us."

"Not all of them will fight to protect us," Sam said, "and some just wallow in self-pity. I suspect, if Zeus offered them a chance to come back, to be restored... some of them would take it."

"But then, they're dangerous. Why let them into Nevah at all?"

"That's the argument. Mist wants to execute all of them, as prisoners of war. Able thinks they're harmless. They were made with Zeus's energy, so they don't age, but they also can't draw on more energy, which makes them weak. Weak, compared to Able. They're still worth ten or twenty men in battle, and half as strong as a hunter. Even if only a handful of torches fight with us, it can make a difference. A torch can play defense and keep a hunter busy for an hour. At least that's the argument Able used the last time we brought it up. But ultimately, it's his decision."

"A few have lost their will to live," Sitri said, "and they're depressing to be around. But many of them are eager to prove their worth and value. Perhaps especially because of the distrust they've been shown here."

"They're a little like dogs," Sam said with a shrug. "They were made to serve. Without a master, they waste away."

I saw Sitri's muscles tense at the comment, and a dark look crossed his face, but he recovered quickly.

"This is Eligor," Sitri introduced me when we reached the torch. From up close, I could see how the burn scars distorted the tattoos on his arms, forming grotesque, ghostly patches of ink and flesh. It looked like he'd put them in a barrel of acid. Unlike Puriel's golden yellow eyes, Eligor's were black with dark orange patches that sparkled like crystals. They looked scorched—like they were filled with smoke and burning embers.

"Eligor, this is Kaidance," Sitri said. Eligor gave me a nod that was almost a bow. He was draped in simple, dark fabrics that looked almost like a robe, held together by a leather belt. "She's a complete beginner, and we want to teach her to fight hunters."

Eligor frowned. "She has an ability, I presume?" Strapped to his back was a black sword that hung down to his knees. It was so long it could have passed for a hockey stick.

"Let's pretend she doesn't," Sam said.

Eligor said nothing, but motioned us to follow behind him. We took a dirt path away from the crowds. At the top of the hill it disappeared into the woods, and we entered single file. The temperature dropped a few degrees immediately. I was glad I'd put on a sweater earlier. Large gray boulders were spread out among the trees. We passed several before I noticed something was off about them and started looking closer. My eyes widened when I saw that one of them had fingers. It was a giant hand, with a thumb so large I couldn't wrap my arms around it.

"This place gets weirder every day," I said, examining the hand. I wiped away a layer of dirt and moss until I could see the aged bronze surface. I tapped on it with my knuckle, and it rang like a gong.

"That's the Colossus of Rhodes," Sam said. "Destroyed in an earthquake in 226 BC. Able had the pieces moved here. I think he planned to restore it, but standing it up would be too conspicuous. I like it this way. It's a reminder of our past."

I marveled at the enormous pieces of the fallen giant as our path wove between them. It seemed like the carcass of a god, being slowly devoured by the teeth of the forest. I wondered if the Statue of Liberty would look like this in a few thousand years.

We had to take a wide detour around the shoulders to reach the head. In front of the huge broken face was a wide meadow, filled with about twenty standing practice dummies.

"Heph designed these," Sam said, approaching the nearest. "Good for basic swordplay." It was holding a beam of wood straight out in front it. Sam knocked it to the side, and the wood beam came back to the center again. Sam kicked the dummy. It bounced off the ground and righted itself.

The dummies had a spongy red ball where the heart should be, and another on the top half of their heads.

"This is basically how it'll work," Sitri said, leaning across from me and pulling my sword out of its scabbard. "And remember, this is only a last resort, emergency move. You lift the shotgun, squeeze the trigger, fire. Then concentrate, and try to pierce their heart with the sword. Simple. One, Two."

He demonstrated, holding the shotgun in one hand and the sword in the other.

"Start with the sword," Sam said, pulling out his own. "To get through this course, you have to take out all the dummies by stabbing them in the heart and brain. Just face off with one of them for now. Practice your aim. Parry, stab."

He showed me with one of the dummies, knocking the beam of wood to the side and stabbing his sword into its heart. The sword stuck in the spongy material, and when Sam pulled his sword out, the fake heart filled in the hole by itself.

Sitri handed me my sword, and I set the satchel with the shotgun against a nearby rock. They let me practice on my own for a few minutes. I hit the beam to the side, but couldn't stab the heart as the dummy was turning back into position. And when it was straight again, I couldn't reach the heart past the long beam. I tried about a hundred times but the tip of my sword always hit wood.

Sitri came up behind me and grabbed my waist. "You're waiting too long, and coming in too straight." I could feel his firm body behind me as he stepped closer and wrapped his fingers around the handle of my sword, covering my hand. For a moment I wished I wasn't wearing gloves, so I could feel his skin on mine.

"Swing to the side, curve back and stab the heart at an angle. It's one fluid movement, not two." He showed me what he meant in slow motion.

After fifteen minutes of practice, I could hit the heart about a third of the time.

"Keep practicing like that, and you might be ready in a year," Eligor said from behind me. I glared at him.

"Today's not about skill, it's about knowledge," Sitri said. He led me to another dummy in the second row. This one was wearing a metal plate over its chest.

"The hunters might be wearing armor—usually silver trimmed with gold. It's softer than iron, but doesn't leach energy. And it's still pretty damn hard. A very powerful weapon might pierce it, but it's safe to assume you won't be able to. If they're wearing armor, shoot for the head, aim for the eye. If you put a sword through their eye, they'll heal, but they'll be out of the battle. A shotgun blast, point blank in the head, might be enough to finish them."

Sitri handed me the shotgun, and showed me how to load it and turn off the safety. "Keep the barrel down. Don't point it at anything you don't want to kill," he said. He held the shotgun with his left hand and a sword in his right. "If you get trapped by a hunter, and he's coming for you, shoot him in the chest—or the head if you're sure you won't miss." Sitri pulled the trigger and the shotgun blasted the dummy backwards. As it bounced back up, Sitri put the sword through its eye and left it there.

"Your turn," he said, handing me the shotgun. "Remember, you only get one chance at it. If you miss, you'll die. But no pressure." He put a foot against the dummy and pulled out his sword, wiping it against his leg. The shotgun was awkward in my left hand. I stood right in front of the dummy, tightened my grip, and squeezed the trigger. The recoil threw my elbow into my stomach, knocking the wind out of me. The dummy bounced off the ground and attacked me with its wooden beam, pushing me off my feet.

I heard laughter and turned to see Mist enter the field, followed by Dion and Tori. "Isn't that adorable," Mist said. "She thinks she can fight a hunter, but she can't even beat the dummy."

"We're just showing her the basics," Sam said. Mist knocked two arrows and fired them at the same time. I flinched as they whizzed over me and thudded into the dummy I was facing, sticking out of its head where its eyes should be. "She might have a better chance if he was blind," Mist said.

"We just came to get a little practice," Dion said. He was holding a long staff and leaned it casually against his neck. Tori was wearing bright red lipstick and some lightweight armor that put her cleavage on display, under a flowing white gown. I wondered how she could keep so clean out here in the woods—my shoes were muddy from the hike in. She fixed me with her mesmerizing eyes and approached, swaying her hips like a cobra. She kissed me on the cheek, just as I felt the blade from a concealed knife scrape against my neck.

"The boys won't teach you everything you need to know," she whispered with a smile. "Including the most important—as a woman, you can distract and charm. Most men will underestimate you, or hesitate from killing you. If you have to fight, use your natural advantages." She ran her fingers over the outside of my sweater, grazing the side of my breast, and winked at me.

"You know that stuff doesn't work on hunters," Mist said. "Besides, it takes too long. Why seduce them when you can skewer them?"

"They understand lust," Tori said. "And they were made to appreciate beauty. Isn't that right, torch?" She wrapped her arms around Eligor and squeezed his butt. He shifted uncomfortably.

"I don't know how you can stand to be that close to one of them," Mist said, turning up her nose. "They're so creepy. And they were made to kill us."

"But *this* one didn't," Sitri said. "Don't you get that yet? He's here because he refused. And he has a name, by the way."

"Doesn't matter. We'll never be able to trust them. What if Zeus lets them come back, but only if they kill ten heirs? Or a hundred? Don't tell me they wouldn't scramble back to him."

"For myself, personally, I could not. And I imagine the other torches are the same, though I cannot speak for them all," Eligor said stiffly.

"You dare talk to me?" Mist said, her eyes burning with fury. Lightning flashed in the distance, followed by the rumble of thunder.

Sitri and Heph moved in front of Eligor warily.

"Whatever. I'm going back in the house if you're going to play with vermin." She spit on the ground, glaring at me.

"No, you stay." Sitri said. "We were just leaving. Besides, the weather has turned."

We walked back to the house through a light rain. I fell in step next to Eligor. I understood Mist's comment about torches being creepy. The dark shadows around their eyes made them look like zombies—like life had buried them and they'd crawled up through the ashes. It was especially noticeable next to the freakishly good-looking members of Able's family. When we exited the woods, I could see several dozen of them, spread out around the house like sentries.

"I don't understand, you're here to help them, to protect them, even though they say bad things about you?" I asked him.

"I don't work for them, I work for Able. Able offered me a place here, and I promised to serve and protect him when needed. I cannot go against my word. It would be a fate worse than death."

"What do you mean?"

"One doubt opens the way to uncertainty. Suddenly, questions become possible. But if we question everything, more and more truths are undone. Some torches keep digging, relentless, unsatisfied. They burn everything, until they believe in nothing and no one, and become shadows of themselves. They are husks—empty shells. We call them roaches, because they are like insects."

"They're hardly conscious, apart from a ferocious despair and anger, and which drives them to suck out every little bit of magic or happiness from the world—an echo of the command which destroyed them, the command we first refused. That command we refused on accident. I can't explain it, it just felt *wrong*. When I was cast off, and Able offered sanctuary, I swore myself to him. He was my life raft. He offered me purpose. If I break that promise, if I defile my honor again—intentionally this time—I'd be lost to myself. I could break more promises. Start lying. Each moral question becomes a dangerous choice; perhaps the last choice I make before becoming a roach myself."

We split up once we reached the house, and left Eligor behind with some other torches. Sitri excused himself to go find Able. Sam took me back to Stephanie's room. We passed through the armory, and waved at Matt and Priya. Their faces were flushed and they looked guilty; I bet we'd almost caught them making out. My clothes were wet from the rain, so I changed them quickly, pulling on a pair of dark jeans and a burgundy hooded sweatshirt. My dark gloves were a little dirty from the outside training, but I pulled them on anyway. At least they were lightweight. Sam waited outside my room, then escorted me upstairs.

Stephanie's room looked different than I remembered it. Against the wall was a black sarcophagus with gold leaf decoration and hieroglyphs, showing a young woman with dark bangs, and there were two onyx statues of tall, black cats I don't remember seeing before. It smelled like incense and jasmine.

Stephanie had changed her appearance to match. She was wearing thick eyeliner and blue eye shadow, with a thin band of shiny gold under each eye. Her hair was up in a bun, and held in place by several long golden needles. Instead of the pretty youth she'd seemed last time, today she was dressed as a dark mistress, and looked devastatingly beautiful.

She prepared a pot of tea and poured two glasses. I waited for mine to cool.

"Learn anything useful?" she said, nodding at the sword.

"Yeah. As long as all the hunters stand perfectly still and let me stab them, I'll be fine."

"Nobody expected you to learn how to fight in one day," Stephanie said. "The sword is a last resort. We have something else for you, to make sure you don't have to use it."

She grabbed a stocking cap from the table near the window held it up to me. It was made of thick, black yarn.

"Um, thanks?"

She put the cap on her head, and disappeared.

"Well actually, it's my husband's," her voice continued, though I could no longer see her. "It's a very old form of magic. And rare. I just made its current form. The magic is in the yarn."

"Invisibility?" I asked.

Stephanie pulled off the cap and tossed it to me. I caught it in one hand, rubbing the fibers between my fingertips.

"Wear it as much as you can, even while you're sleeping. And take this as well." She reached behind her slender neck and undid the clasp to her necklace—a glittering design with flat links of gold framing a handful of large red rubies.

"I've been wearing it since last night, so it's charged with my energy. If you keep the stones against your skin, you should heal as quickly as Able or I."

I put my palm to my chest and felt the bump of my necklace against my collarbone. I took it off and put it in my pocket carefully. Stephanie moved behind me, lifting up my hair so she could fasten the necklace. I felt a surge of power as it touched my skin, and my eyes widened.

"You'll feel stronger and faster with it on," Stephanie said. "But don't let it fool you. You're still weak compared to the hunters, and with zero skill there is no way you'd survive a fight. When they come, you disappear and let us deal with them."

"It doesn't feel right," I said. "It feels selfish to sit back and let other people protect me. Die for me. I don't want to be the cause of any more death."

Stephanie laughed harshly. "As if they would die for *you*. But if you feel bad about it, learn to control your gift."

"But how?" I asked.

"Genetic heritage usually activates when life is threatened. We've tried that with you, so we have some sense of what you're capable of. Now you need to learn to do it intentionally. Pain is the fastest way to sharpen focus." She pulled one of the golden needles out of her bun.

"I studied medicine for a while, you know. I was never as good as Alice, but I did find one thing useful. The practical application of pain. This little needle, through an eyeball or a testicle, under a kneecap or fingernail, into a kidney or liver, can cause considerably more anguish than your sword. And I could kill you with it in a hundred different ways. If you want to truly know yourself, explore the boundaries of your pain."

She handed me the needle. Goose pimples raised over my skin. What did she expect me to do, torture myself?

"When I was a young girl," Stephanie said, "I fell in love." She turned her back on me and returned to her flower arrangement.

"His name was Peirithous, and he was my whole world. We planned to marry as soon as we were old enough. Then one day I was out picking flowers, and I heard thunder—but it was the galloping of mighty hooves. A magnificent carriage pulled up next to me, and out stepped the most handsome man I'd ever seen, wrapped in a thick dark cloak. He swept me off my feet. What can I say, I was a poor country girl and he was a cultured stranger. I was captivated."

"Able?" I asked. Stephanie nodded.

"We ran away together, and got married in secret. He bought me a fine house and gave me everything I'd ever wanted. I figured Peirithous would forget about me, but he didn't. My mother and all my friends convinced him I'd been abducted against my will. He came after me, to rescue me."

"When he arrived, I was too ashamed to speak with him. My husband invited him in and had him sit on a stone chair, but he cursed it first. The stone seat enveloped Peirithous and turned him to stone."

"Why would Able do that?" I asked.

"Jealousy. Spite. Or just for a passing moment of entertainment. We were all capricious back then. Mortals meant little to us. Later, when Zeus took over, he killed my mother—his own sister. She wasn't a warrior, she was just a woman. A gardener. If I'd have stayed home, maybe I could have protected her. Saved her. Instead I'd run away with Able, leaving her all alone. And Zeus killed her. First my lover, then my mother. One killed by my husband, the other killed by his brother."

She turned around to face me, her eyes flashing with anger.

"So I don't care how guilty you feel about your dead brother, or how selfish you feel being protected by us. You don't matter at all. I'm doing this because my first love was cut down, and dried up and turned to ash in my mouth, and because I'll never again taste the sweetness of youth without biting into the bitterness of regret."

Her pupils were black voids, rimmed with a line of ice blue that flickered like fire. A breeze tore through the room, causing the shutters to slam and a painting to fall off the wall. Stephanie's dress flared out behind her, and her voice grew larger, more powerful. Shadows flew around the room, cast by an unseen source. Her voice dropped several octaves, and roared through the room.

"I have caused death. I have lived it. All the while, I've been waiting for the instrument of my revenge. If that's you, the sniveling girl standing in front of me, I'll use it. Because those I've lost to Zeus deserve justice. And because of that, I protect you—but make no mistake, it's not because I care what happens to you. And if I need to hurt you to make you stronger, rest assured I will do what's necessary."

I cringed, and Stephanie seemed to calm down. She straightened her dress and redid her bun, taking the golden needle back from me and sticking it into her dark hair.

"The more you lose, the stronger you get. But you might be our only chance to win this war. So when they come for you, don't do anything stupid. You put the cap on, and you hide. Got it?"

I nodded, then reached for the teapot on the table with shaky fingers and poured myself a cup. I'd just taken a sip, savoring the taste and aroma of the tea, when a blinding flash of lightning evaporated the ceiling.

15

The tea cup shattered against the floor. The lightning bolt had pierced through the ceiling with tremendous force, sending a cascade of sizzling stone and charred wood down on us. I looked up into the rain to see four more bolts of lightning. Wait, not lightning. I could see figures in the flashes. *Hunters.*

They tumbled into the room, weapons drawn. Stephanie killed two of them before they took their first step. I heard a high pitched whine as her golden needles found their marks. The other two fell between us. "Run!" Stephanie shouted. I could barely hear her above the roaring wind.

I dashed out of the room with a hunter right behind me as Stephanie faced off with the other. I raced around a corner and pulled on the stocking cap, then flattened myself against the wall. The hunter sailed past me. I held my breath as he paused and looked back at me, narrowing his eyes. His wings shimmered like liquid mirrors behind him. Then he kept going. I was invisible.

I was supposed to head to Able's study and hide in his secret room behind his bookshelf. But I could hear shouting and fighting in either direction. The best thing to do would be to stay put and hide. I ducked into the corner next to a window. I could see what was happening outside, while also watching the hall.

I saw Stephanie leave her room and head downstairs. Another hunter crept in from the right. They were dressed identically, with form-fitting, heavily decorated armor so shiny it gave off a ghostly glow. I held my breath as he passed me. Two torches charged up the stairs and attacked him with fury. The hunter's wings folded behind him, like a shimmering cloak. His long sword sizzled with blue energy. Soon the torches were lagging. They were going to lose.

I pulled the shotgun out of my bag, careful not to make any noise. If I could get close enough to shoot the hunter, it might distract him long enough for one of the torches to finish him off. I crouched in the corner clutching the shotgun, my heart pounding, looking for an opening—but the flashes of steel, the thunderous din of battle petrified me. It was way too fast. And Stephanie had told me to stay hidden.

The hunter slashed through one of the torch's legs, disconnecting it from his body just below the knee. Thick, black blood oozed out of the wound like tar. The hunter turned and stabbed the torch behind him in the heart with lethal accuracy, then spun and decapitated the one standing on one leg. Both bodies fell to the ground. I felt dizzy and thought I smelled vomit. It might have been my own. The smell reminded me of Dennis. I realized I hadn't thought about him much since I'd been here, and I felt bad about it. When you see someone murdered in front of you, you should remember.

"She was with Stephanie, she must be up here!" a voice shouted. Matt's voice. I put my hand over my mouth to keep from shouting a warning. As the hunter turned towards the stairs, a beam of light illuminated his face. Now that he'd stopped moving, I realized that I recognized him. *Puriel.* His noble, strong features made him look like royalty in his gold and silver armor. He flicked his sword, and it tossed a splatter of black blood against the wall. It looked like an ink blot test. Part of me wanted to stare at it until I saw something meaningful.

The other part of me watched, in horror, as Priya and Matt raced up the stairs towards him. Priya was nearly invisible in her camouflage. I saw a flash of a blade as she hurled herself at Puriel. He caught her easily by the neck and threw her aside violently.

Matt sprouted a pair of horns and charged at Puriel, ramming him with his shoulder. He pushed the hunter across the hall and lifted him up with his horns, pinning him against the wall. Puriel's blood sparkled like silver glitter and I saw him gasp in pain.

He reached up, then smashed his elbow downwards so hard he broke through Matt's horn. He tore the horn out of his own stomach and tossed it aside. Puriel's sword flared with energy, heating up like molten metal, and he pressed it against his own abdomen. I heard his flesh sizzle as the wound sealed itself.

Then he kicked off the wall, forcing Matt backwards, and swung his sword. It caught Matt in the chest. He fell, trying to hold the bloody gash together with his palms. Priya jumped on Puriel and slashed her knives across his face. He smacked her with the back of his hand. She flew into the wall and crumpled in a heap.

The wounds on Puriel's face starting sealing themselves as he walked over to Matt and pointed his sword at his chest. It was exactly like the sword I'd seen in my vision.

"Where is she?" he said. "Tell me or die."

"No!" I shouted, tearing off the invisibility cap and stepping into the light. "Don't kill him!"

Puriel looked at me, eyes widening, and hesitated. And that hesitation became a pause, which became a look of abject horror. And then he started screaming. His wings, which had been scarcely visible before, burst into fire. The rushing sounds of his screams and the flames filled the hall with an unearthly shriek. I covered my ears against the noise.

Puriel's whole upper body was on fire now, and I could see that his arms were burning too—the dark lines of his tattoos were glowing like embers, and I could smell burning flesh. He looked like one of the roman candle fireworks we had once for the Fourth of July, back when I was young. I remember my dad holding our little fingers, me on his right, my brother on his left. I was five, my brother was three. For some reason as I stood there, stunned, watching Puriel burn, I recalled that memory with perfect clarity.

Through the smoke, I saw Sitri and Heph approaching Puriel warily with their swords. He was smoking and steaming now, but most of the fire had gone out. His arms were covered in nasty burns that obscured the tattoos. He bowed his head as the others restrained him, and I thought I heard him sobbing. I rushed past him to join Priya on the floor with Matt, holding my breath. Joy filled me when I saw his chest rise. He was breathing. He was still alive.

16

Sitri grabbed me and practically carried me back to my room. I tried to walk, but my legs were trembling—adrenaline was still pumping through my body. The smell of burning feathers seemed to follow me. I wondered if it was in my clothes, and the thought made my skin crawl.

"Stay here!" Sitri said, shoving me inside. He ordered four torches to guard my door. When I tried to leave, they crossed their long, dark swords and blocked my path. *Was I a prisoner now?*

I couldn't stop thinking about Puriel. Why didn't he kill me when he had the chance? Why had he caught on fire like that? I was desperate to talk to Sitri or Able—I knew they'd have answers. From the window of my room, I could see the torches begin cleaning up the wreckage from the house, and carrying out the bodies—long shapes wrapped in white sheets, with black stains I now knew was torch blood. I was most worried about Matt and Priya. The slash across Matt's chest looked lethal, and the last I saw of Priya she was nearly unconscious. I wondered how many others were injured. Being stuck in my room was driving me crazy. I should be out there, helping.

An hour passed before I realized I still had Able's invisibility cap—I'd stuck it in my pocket after confronting Puriel. Maybe it took that long to calm down after my near-death experience and start thinking clearly again. That's when I realized the full significance of what had happened.

A few days ago I'd had a vision of Matt's death. I saw the sword sticking out of his beastly chest, blood gurgling from his lips. The golden sword, glittering with blue jewels; the crown that symbolized Zeus's kingdom shining like a beacon in the darkness. All of Zeus's winged army had swords like that—hunters, created to rid the world of magic.

In the past, every time I had a vision of someone's death, it came true. But this time was different. When hunters broke in through the ceiling like bolts of lightning, it was my death they were after. I couldn't let Matt die for me. And I also couldn't bring myself to use the shotgun and sword Sitri had given me, like I was supposed to. Not when I saw Puriel. His tall, muscular body. His amber eyes and nearly white hair. The shimmering mirrored wings behind him. *How could I destroy something that beautiful?* I didn't want any more violence. I just wanted it to stop. I didn't have a plan, but in that moment, I thought I was going to die.

Instead, Puriel burst into flames, and Matt lived. Which means, *my visions don't have to come true.* Which means, *I might not be the monster everyone always thought I was.* This realization made my heart pound with excitement. My world seemed to grow larger with all the new possibilities. If what I saw didn't have to come true, that meant I could warn people. Save people. Like I'd wanted to save my brother.

But why did Puriel hesitate? Why not destroy me like Zeus ordered him to? He'd become a torch, cast off from Zeus's favor. After serving obediently for thousands of years. How could that have happened?

I had to find out. I snuck through the bathroom into Sitri's room and opened the door cautiously. With the cap on I stuck my head out to peek at the torches guarding my room. The floorboard creaked when I took my first step and I froze as two torches whipped their heads towards me. I thought my heart was beating loud enough for them to hear it, but after a moment they faced forward again like marble statues. I waited until their dark robes were perfectly still before walking down the hall and turning the corner.

Most of the mansion was empty. I was surprised there wasn't more damage. It seemed the attack was focused only on the upstairs floors—as if they knew exactly where I would be. I heard voices and followed them to the second level, where I found Eligor addressing a small group of torches.

"The threat was neutralized quickly—ten hunters drew attention away from the main building by starting skirmishes around the defensive barrier, just as four breached the top floor. Two lost their lives immediately. Apparently they didn't expect to find Stephanie there, or underestimated her power. The third was killed soon after. The fourth, captured."

"Is it true the fourth hunter fell?" someone asked. There were murmurs when Eligor nodded. He held a hand up and continued.

"I don't know what it means yet, nor should we be overly curious. We should also not assume, now fallen, he will join our ranks—the fate of the intruder will be decided by Able and the masters of Nevah, and we will accept their decision without question. For now, he's being held in the dungeon until decisions are made. We should also not assume the threat is over. Zeus's army didn't get what they came for, this time. They will undoubtedly strike again soon with double the force. Be vigilant."

What they came for... my skin prickled as I realized he was talking about me. It wasn't over. They'd come back, and more people could die next time.

Eligor gave instructions and the torches left to carry them out. He hesitated when we were alone, his fingers reaching up for the hilt of his sword, and looked at the place where I was standing. But then he left and I was alone.

I wandered lower and lower into the house until I found a room I hadn't been in before. In the corner was a descending spiral staircase made of large rectangular slabs of stone. I followed it down into a sublevel of the complex, which looked practically medieval. Furnaces and fireplaces cast a glowing light between large sections of inky darkness.

I went down a long hall full of canned goods and emergency supplies. It looked like Nevah had enough food and supplies stockpiled to last a hundred years. I shuddered as I passed a room full of hooks, chains and complex devices I hoped weren't tools of torture. Finally, after exploring a dozen labyrinthine passageways, I found a row of thick iron doors with tiny barred windows. I peeked in the rooms until I found Puriel.

I could barely see him in the dark. His pale, white body made him look like a ghost, surrounded by walls of solid concrete. Ash and soot stuck to his skin in dark patches, and he smelled like singed hair and burnt feathers. I heard the grating noise of heavy chains being dragged across the stone floor and noticed that the dark cuffs around his neck and wrists were fixed to the wall.

I gasped when he looked up. His eyes were black sockets—gaping voids of desolation and heartbreak. The beautiful creature Puriel had been was gone, and the figure before me was ruin incarnate. His eyes sparked like glowing coals—furious patches of bright orange that burned in the darkness of the room. He moaned, straining against his restraints, his muscles tensed as he reached towards the door. Towards me.

I choked back a sob at the thing he'd become.

I found a set of skeleton keys hanging on a hook several doors down, and turned each one until I felt the lock click.

"It's you, isn't it?" Puriel said as the door creaked open. His eyes darted across the cell. I realized he still couldn't see me. I stepped into the far corner of the room, out of his reach, and removed Able's invisibility cap.

"Come to torment me further? Survey your handiwork?" he said bitterly.

"I didn't mean for this to happen to you. Whatever *this* is... I was just trying to save my friend."

"And that's exactly why I fell. A cruel trick. A mean trick. But so what, it's over now. I'm here, a prisoner without purpose, without hope, condemned forever to waste away in suffering and darkness."

"Why were you after me? I've never done anything to you. You chased me from JDRI. Then you followed me here," I accused. "Why?"

"I don't ask why. My Lord commands and I obey."

"You mean Zeus?" I asked. Everything Able told me had been true.

""Zeus is his pagan name," he spat. "We use his Latin name, *Deus*. The one true king. Pure goodness and perfection. My maker and master. Whom I have faithfully served since he gave me life. Until today, when I failed him."

"Failed him, by not killing me?"

Puriel nodded, then sank his face in his hands. My fingers dragged against the rough stone wall behind me as I waited for him to speak again.

"I hesitated, because I thought I saw goodness in you, and it made me doubt. Now I understand that you are the worst kind of evil. The kind that thinks they are good, but doesn't know any better. You lie so perfectly I saw no trace of deceit or malice in you. Only innocence, kindness, courage—"

"Zeus is the evil one," I said. "He slaughtered his own family. Able told me all about it."

"*Able,*" Puriel repeated with a sad smile, "has told you nothing but lies. Even the name he's given himself, it sounds so ordinary. So innocuous. It hides the truth of what he really is."

"And what is he?" I asked nervously.

"He has many names. Father of Lies. Prince of Darkness. Ruler of the Underworld. In French he's called *Le Diable*."

My knees trembled as the word resonated in the small cell. I'd heard those titles before... but they didn't make any sense here. Those were names for the devil. What did that have to do with Greek mythology? My stomach twisted in knots as I realized Puriel was telling the truth. *Le Diable—Able.* I'd dined with the devil and didn't even know it. Suddenly, everything clicked into place. The hunters could fly and had wings. They served their almighty lord with pure obedience.

"You're an *angel*," I said, breathlessly.

"Some humans call us that," he said. "We prefer the term *seraphim*. We burn with the inexhaustible energy of Deus, like mirrors reflecting his power and glory." He looked down at his hands in wonder, turning them over slowly. "I *was* seraphim. Now I am nothing. Cast out. Defective. A broken vessel. Yesterday I could have melted through these chains."

I felt sorry for him, even though he had been trying to kill me. In a twisted way, he'd sacrificed himself to save me. Even if he hadn't done it on purpose, and even if he was regretting it now, I still felt a twinge of responsibility. My head was spinning as I reached for the door handle. I was overcome with confusing emotions, and the stone walls of the cramped space felt like they were closing in. My throat tightened and I felt like I couldn't breathe. *I had to get out of here.*

"Deus does not explain himself to the seraphim," he said quietly as I was leaving, "nor do we try to understand his will. But I can share what he called you, the name he used when he gave the order. *Deicidium*. From *Deus*, meaning *god* and *cidium*, which means cutting. In English, it would translate as *godkiller*. You should ask Able, when you see him again, why you're really here."

* * *

I retraced my footsteps until I found my way back upstairs. I wondered if anybody even knew I was missing yet. My head felt like it was going to explode. In every story I'd ever heard, angels were the good guys. And one just tried to kill me.

Able told me stories about the Greek Parthenon. He'd hinted that some of the gods of Olympus were still harbored at Nevah, rather than just heirs and descendants. But which ones? And who was who? Most importantly, whose house was I really in, and was I even safe here? After what I'd learned from Puriel, I wasn't sure who I could trust anymore.

There was one room where I'd find answers. It took me awhile to find it—the house was a maze that almost seemed to shift around. But finally I noticed the gleam of blue light under a door at the end of a dark corridor, and entered the room where I'd seen the massive indoor temple. Inside, the giant statues stood just as I'd left them, surrounding the glowing tree. Only this time I looked closely at their faces.

The last time I'd been in here, I still thought of these as mythical archetypes. Imaginary legends. But if Zeus was real, not to mention trying to kill me, the other figures in this room could be real, too. I realized each statue had a small marker in glowing blue letters. I could have sworn they were in Greek the first time I was here, but now I could read them clearly.

Athena and Hera, I'd never met. Zeus's head was missing but he wouldn't be at Nevah anyway.

Able said that Zeus had killed Poseidon and Apollo, and Athena had treacherously defeated Ares. I found their statues, and noticed this time that freshly cut flowers—roses and irises—had been placed in vases in front of them. The sweetly floral scent made me light headed.

Opposite Zeus, towering above the door I'd come through but hidden in shadows, was a statue of Hades that I hadn't noticed last time. Though the statue was sporting luxuriously curled locks of hair and a heavy beard, it had more than a passing resemblance to Able.

To his right was Persephone, goddess of the spring, and the wife of Hades. A dead-ringer for Stephanie. Heph was Hephaestus, the smithing god, son of Zeus and Hera. Mist was Artemis, goddess of the moon and the hunt—twin sister of Apollo. Dion was Dionysus, god of wine; Tori was Aphrodite, goddess of love. I even found Sam—Zeus's youngest son and Apollo's little brother Hermes, messenger of the gods, with wings on his feet and helmet.

It was so obvious. I felt stupid for not figuring it out sooner. I didn't see Alice or Sitri. The last statue was Demeter, with flowing robes and holding a cornucopia. From what I remembered of Greek mythology, she was a nature goddess and Persephone's mother. So there they were. The gods of Olympus. Four were dead, three were out to kill me, and I'd been living with the remaining seven for the past week.

I felt the hair rise on my arms and I shivered. This room felt several degrees cooler than the rest of the house. I heard breathing and realized someone was behind me. I spun around just as Able started speaking.

"There were only twelve actual Olympians, as I'm sure you knew. Living on their holy mountain, cut off from the real world. They didn't count Stephanie and I. We preferred to live among the humans. By the way, you can't hide from me. It is my invisibility cap after all. Hand it back please."

Able looked guarded, as if he was expecting me to refuse. I saw his muscles tense under his navy jacket. He looked flawless as always, with his polished black shoes and tailored white shirt—like he'd just gotten off a yacht somewhere. But after what I'd seen Stephanie do to those two torches, I knew I had no chance of resisting him. I slowly took the cap off and handed it back with trembling fingers. I tried to keep my face from betraying my fear. I knew challenging him was stupid, and I should keep my mouth shut… but I was tired of secrets.

"You lied to me," I accused. "You're Hades. Lord of the Underworld."

"I've told you nothing but the truth since you got here," Able sighed, running a hand through his hair. He seemed disappointed with me, like I was a slow student and he'd reached the end of his rope.

"Should I have used the name my enemy gave me, a name he spent thousands of years dragging through the mud, trying to turn me into something I'm not?"

"You deny it? That you're the devil? Evil incarnate?" My eyes flicked to his forehead to check for horns. He noticed and rolled his eyes.

"Those are just words. I'm as much pure evil as Zeus is pure good—a myth he keeps trying to get humans to believe. Each individual is only as good or evil as the choices they make, and the people they hurt."

"But why lie about it? Why not just tell me the truth from the beginning?"

"What would you do if people only referred to you in derogatory nomenclatures. *Bitch. Slut. Whore.* They've called Tori these and worse. Would you accept their opinions of you as truth? Or try to prove them wrong? I find it's easier for people to get to know me if they don't already have all of that propaganda in their ears."

My lips moved but I couldn't think of anything to say. I couldn't believe this conversation was even happening. Able continued when I didn't respond.

"Lord of the Underword? I never wanted that job. We drew lots. Zeus got the sky, Poseidon got the sea, and I got the earth, and what's below it. And I'm pretty sure Zeus cheated. It's been my job to care for humanity, both the living and the dead—but I did it my way. Quietly. When Zeus decided to clean up his image and wield universal power by destroying all other sources of magic, he turned me into a monster. All gods and heirs became devils and demons. All of our gifts became suspect. Miraculous healings, objects of power, special abilities—every time we tried to help the humans, Zeus's hunters, or sometimes the humans themselves, would destroy our best work."

"So you rebelled," I said.

"If you mean, when Zeus tried to murder his entire family so he could become sole arbiter of power, I offered them protection and shelter, yes I *rebelled.* And I'd do it again in a heartbeat. One third of Zeus's own army, which he'd built to have unquestionable loyalty, still turned away from him and sided with us. You think it would be anywhere near that number if there hadn't been truth in our cause? His own army refused him."

My temple was throbbing. *The devil was defending himself to me, and I was starting to believe him.* Able's arguments made sense, but I was still wary. Under his carefully polished image, the designer clothes and trimmed beard, I could sense how powerful he was, and something else—how much he wanted me to trust him. He was practically desperate for my approval. But that didn't make any sense. What would the devil need from me?

"Why did you really bring me here?" I asked. I realized too late I was repeating Puriel's words exactly. "What do you want from me, from my abilities?"

There was a long pause as Able considered my question. The flickering blue lights in the room made his features slip around his face, like a mask that was about to fall off.

"Why *do you* think I brought you here?" he asked finally.

"Puriel called me *Deicidium*. Is that why I'm here? To kill Zeus?"

He looked confused for a moment.

"Puriel—you mean the hunter? You know its name? *You spoke with him*?" Able's last sentence boomed in the cavernous space and the rivers of blue light crackled with energy. Able clenched his fist and took a deep breath.

"I need a drink," he said, massaging his forehead. He spun and left the room, leaving me behind him. Without his presence, the marble statues seemed ominous and disapproving. I hesitated before following after him. I had the impulse to run, and get as far away from this place as possible. But I also needed answers. Able didn't seem to have any intention of hurting me. Unlike Zeus, who was obviously not trying to be my friend. For the moment, I seemed safer here than anywhere else. I found Able in his office and watched him pour two glasses full of whiskey. He offered one to me, then drank the other in one gulp.

In Able's cozy office my anxiety lessened. Able still looked like a handsome college professor, at home with his books. No horns, no tail, no pitchfork. I'd never believed in that kind of devil anyway, why start now?

Able sank into his leather couch and leaned back. I took a seat in one of the cushioned antique chairs with ornately carved armrests. The red leather felt cool against my back. I took a sip of the whiskey and it burned my throat. Suddenly I felt exhausted. I realized I'd been running on adrenaline for several hours. I was still wearing the hooded sweatshirt I'd put on to meet Stephanie, but it smelled like sweat.

"I brought you here," Able said slowly, holding my gaze with his dark, stormy eyes, "because Zeus was trying to kill you. Just like he killed Poisedon, our brother; my nephews Apollo and Ares; and thousands of others. I brought you here so you'd be safe, just like all of the others I've taken under my protection. Am I also curious about you, about what you can do for us, about why my brother fears you enough to attack my household directly, for the first time in over a thousand years? Yes, obviously, and I won't apologize for it." He poured another glass of whiskey, and this time swirled the amber liquid in the glass before taking a sip. Then he took a deep breath and leaned back in his chair.

"I have a duty to all the inhabitants of Nevah, and having you here puts them in danger. For now, at the very least, I'm keeping you away from Zeus until we figure out why you're so important to him. So I sincerely hope you'll do us a favor, and next time they come for you, you'll do as I say and stay hidden."

"You think they'll come back? Try again... for me?" I shuddered. First Zeus sent Puriel, alone, to JDRI. This time, according to Eligor, he'd sent at least fourteen hunters after me. What if next time it was one hundred? A thousand? I couldn't imagine that kind of force tearing through Nevah.

"Yes, and soon," Able said, confirming my fears.

"But why keep me here at all? If I'm putting people at risk, why not send me away?"

"Because," Able said, "until we know exactly what you're capable of or why Zeus is so interested in you, you may be more dangerous to us dead than alive."

I gulped, trying to make sense of that statement. Able was keeping me alive because Zeus was trying to kill me—and if Zeus wanted me dead, that meant I was a threat to him, somehow. So Able was trying to use me. Keeping me alive until he figured out what I could do for him.

But so what? If I had to pick sides, shouldn't I pick the side that was motivated to *keep me alive*? My brain was getting fuzzy as the whiskey relaxed me. Even my eyelids were starting to feel heavy and I blinked to keep them open.

"I'm going to sleep," I said suddenly, putting my empty glass down on the table. "I need some time to process all of this."

Able looked surprised and raised his eyebrows. "You're staying?" he said, appraising me with interest. "Even after knowing what I am? Most people would be plotting their escape." There was a touch of sadness in his eyes. I imagined what it would be like, trying to protect and take care of humanity when they treated you like a monster.

"Am I a prisoner?" I asked.

"I won't force you to stay, even though allowing you to leave could cost us the war."

"But I'm safer here, surrounded by torches, than I would be out there on my own, right?"

"Infinitely."

"Then we can talk again in the morning."

I stood up to leave but paused at the door.

"Why Able?" I asked. "Is it just because it's short for *Diable*?"

"Partly. And also because it refers to possibility and action, being *able* to do something.

But mainly, I chose it from the biblical story. Cain is usually called the first murderer, who killed his brother out of jealousy. Able is the righteous victim, who does nothing to deserve the violence against him. But in my relationship with my brother Zeus, he is the one who killed his brother, not me. Then he killed his own sons. He is more like Cain than I will ever be."

The torches were still in front of my door when I reached my room. They nodded at me in acknowledgment, but their frowns let me know they weren't happy I'd given them the slip. I hoped they wouldn't get in any trouble for not keeping better track of me. The door to the bathroom was open and Sitri was in there, trying to wash his back with a damp rag.

"There you are," he said with relief. "I went looking for you. I heard you talking with Able in his office so I figured you were safe. Are you okay?"

He put a hand on my shoulder and his blue eyes shone with concern. I wished I could melt into him and let him wrap his arms around me. At

JDRI I'd always been the strong one—keeping my skin covered up. Closing myself off. Learning to push down the grief over losing my brother, and then being abandoned by my parents. I'd been strong for Jesse, for Sarah. But now I felt like I was unraveling.

I grabbed the damp rag from Sitri and wiped it across his back. I gasped when I saw the rag turn red—deep cuts marred his skin and there were bruises along his arms. I'd almost forgotten he'd been fighting today. *Fighting to protect me.*

"Can't Alice heal you?" I asked.

"She's got her hands full. Most of the beds in the infirmary are taken. I've been down there helping her patch people up."

"How's Matt? Priya? The other heirs? Did they attack the camp too?

"Injured, but they'll heal. Most heirs heal quickly, using their own energy. The torches aren't so lucky. Those that weren't killed will need several days of rest before their wounds close. They have no energy to draw on, so Alice shares hers."

"She can do that?"

"Alice is strong. Much stronger than me. Her Greek name is Aceso. Asclepius was her father. She's Apollo's granddaughter."

I rinsed the blood out in the sink with hot water, then cleaned the deep cuts as gently as I could. I could feel the warmth of Sitri's skin, and his scent was intoxicating. While Able smelled like whiskey, leather and cigars, Sitri smelled like pine needles, the earth after a summer rain and something exotic—like a spice I wasn't familiar with. He'd brought some tape and bandages from downstairs, so I dried him off with a towel and started to cover his wounds. I blushed as I ran my gloved fingertips over his warm skin. Then I pulled away, before he realized I'd already finished bandaging him. When I glanced up I caught him looking at me in the mirror, and my blush deepened. I said goodnight awkwardly and returned to my room.

Even though I was exhausted, it took a while to fall asleep, especially with Sitri in the next room, and the doors open between us. My bed felt too large, the space beside me too empty. The scent of him was still caught in my nostrils.

It grounded me. Thinking about Sitri kept me from thinking about all the other things that were fighting for my attention, like the fact that there was an angel in a cell downstairs that had tried to kill me… and how I'd destroyed him.

17

The next morning, the house was quiet and still. I'd washed my gloves and let them dry overnight. The leather felt soft and cool as I slipped them on. I grabbed a clean white shirt and a beige cardigan, and made my way to the dining room. The impressive breakfast feast looked like it had barely been touched. For the first time I wondered where all this food came from, and who prepared it. After two cups of strong coffee my head was clear and I felt more optimistic than I had last night.

Even though yesterday was a disaster, one thing gave me hope. Matt was still alive. Had my vision been wrong? Or, having seen it, had we prevented it? If so, could I prevent other deaths, by warning more people—by warning *everyone?* If Zeus was going to keep coming after me, I could at least give Able's family a chance to protect themselves. *Forewarned is forearmed.* I couldn't shake my conversation with Puriel, however. With the exception of Mist, most of the inhabitants of Nevah had been kind to me. But what if they were just using me for something? How could I tell whether I was on the right side of things? Was Able really protecting me? Or recruiting me?

It was still early. Outside the light was dim and there was a white fog surrounding the main house. I could barely make out the tall pine trees that led towards the camp. Since nobody else was around, I decided to go check on Matt. I heard laughter and the tinkling of water from the central fountain before I entered the infirmary. I felt uplifted as soon as I entered. Sitri was right, Alice was generous with her power—the whole room felt charged with energy. Sitri was telling a story, waving his hands, and Alice was laughing.

She turned and smiled at me. Not for the first time, I wondered if they were together—then I felt guilty, remembering how I'd helped bandage him up yesterday. Even though nothing had happened, it seemed intimate. For me at least.

Priya was sitting next to Matt's bed, reading a book. Her blue dress brought out the richness of her dark skin. Matt's whole chest was wrapped in white bandages. He smiled when he saw me, and Priya turned her head in my direction. Then she jumped up and pulled me into a tight hug that took my breath away.

"Since he can't hug you yet, I need to do it for the both of us. I was barely conscious, but I saw what you did. I'll never be able to thank you enough."

"I didn't do anything," I said. "You two were incredible, fighting with the torches. I could never have done that."

"All we did was slow them down," Priya said. "And I've got the bruises to prove it." She lifted up her shirt and showed me ugly purple bruises around her ribs.

"But you," Matt said, looking at me in wonder, "You made one *fall*."

"I didn't do it on purpose," I said. "I don't even know what I did, exactly."

"If you figure it out," Sitri said, joining us, "please let us know. We could really use it. Imagine if we could make more hunters turn away from Zeus. Or all of them."

"But seriously, thank you," Priya continued. "You were amazing. That moment, when you appeared out of nowhere, weaponless, palms open, putting yourself between a hunter's blade and Matt... it was the bravest, most impressive thing I've ever seen." Priya's dark eyes were filled with emotion, and it made my own eyes water.

"It was also reckless, and incredibly stupid," Sitri cut in, frowning. "Especially with everyone fighting to protect you."

"And yet nonetheless heroic," Alice corrected, coming up behind him and giving him a look with her gray eyes. "The whole camp is buzzing about it. I think Sam is already writing a song about it. The girl who, with her innocence and beauty, stopped the vengeful sword… or something along those lines."

"We owe you a debt," Matt said.

"If you'll excuse us," Sitri said to the others, "there's something I'd like to show Kaidance." He nodded towards the door and I followed him outside.

We turned right, down a well-worn path I hadn't explored before. Instead of heading into the trees like the path to camp, this one led over the hill to a flat, rocky area and wove between some large boulders. As we climbed higher I could see Nevah spread out behind me—the massive mansion, the amphitheater, and what looked like a sculpted garden. It looked so luxurious and European, I had to keep reminding myself that I was still in Washington state. Somewhere past the tall pine trees that surrounded the estate were ordinary small towns. Gas stations and diners. Schools and hospitals. I felt like I'd fallen off the face of reality and gotten lost in history.

We pushed forward over the top of the hill. Sitri paused and let me take in the view of the other side. It took a minute to fully comprehend what I was seeing. The ground was flat and rocky, and spread out into a wide plain. But just below us was an enormous dark circle. At first I thought it was a lake, or the shadow of the moon. Then I figured out it was just a big hole. A perfectly round hole of epic proportions, with straight walls that disappeared into the earth.

"What is it?" I asked. "A sinkhole?"

"It's where the torches live," Sitri said. "They are sensitive to light. When they first fell, they lived in caves, which they dug and expanded. They became experienced miners and traded gems and gold with the humans. When Able moved his family here, he gave them this land and they built this."

We walked down closer to the hole. It was so big I couldn't have thrown a rock to the other side. Even when we were right at the edge, looking down, I couldn't see the bottom. Four spiral staircases, carved into the walls of the opening, started from each quarter and spun downwards. Far below, lanterns lit up the dark abyss. Most of the walls were smooth, but there were patches of raised relief carvings and decorations. I guessed they were historical scenes, similar to Able's skull carvings but on a massive scale.

"They *live* here?" I asked. "Isn't it a bit... austere?" Compared to the over-the-top luxury of Able's house, or even the camp's comfortable forest village, this place seemed like a less than optimal choice.

"They live simply. Like monks, or a hive almost. Ants maybe. They practice restraint and moderation. They train and fight together. They consider their fall as a kind of rebirth, a baptism of fire. They seek purpose and meaning, through service to Able."

Sitri started down the stairs and I followed him. We walked through cavernous hallways, magnificently sculpted out of the bedrock. They were lit up by flickering candles and oil lanterns.

Down further, the ceiling opened up into chamber that felt like a cathedral, with a high domed ceiling and meticulously painted walls. It was packed with torches, several hundred of them at least. Their ash-blonde hair stood out from their dark robes. It was a ceremony of some kind. I could smell incense, and heard the periodic chime of a very small bell, with a sweet, high-pitched ring.

Then I saw the bodies—laid out on tall slabs of rock. This was a *funeral.* The ceremony was conducted in silence. I watched as torches stepped forward and placed a flower, or a small keepsake next to the body in silence. Private remembrances. Eligor was standing in front of the chapel. When nobody else stepped forward, he nodded to several torches next to him. They pushed the slabs of stone into deep holes that had been cut straight into the rock, slid capstones over the holes, and then filled the seams with wet clay.

"Why did you bring me here?" I asked Sitri.

"It's easy to forget, near Alice. Pain and suffering seem to disappear. People get better. They heal. Only torches died this time. For most of the heirs, the torches are expendable. Able keeps them around precisely for his purpose, to redeem themselves by defending Nevah. But they are also individuals. Each one unique, with stories from a thousand life times—roaming the earth to find pockets of magic, and protect them from

Zeus's hunters. They've fought hundreds of battles for what they believed in. What I mean is, just because it was a torch doesn't mean their death doesn't matter."

His words hit me like a slap and I took a sharp intake of breath. "You think I don't care about them? That I don't realize it's *my* fault they died? The hunters came for me. These torches died protecting me. I get it. But thanks for the reminder, I guess I wasn't feeling shitty enough already." I turned and started walking back the way we came.

"That's not what I meant," Sitri frowned, catching up to me. "I didn't mean that this was your fault. It's not your fault. I just wanted you to *see* them. The hunters are beautiful, powerful, strong. It's easy to see them as *good*. Torches are just the opposite. With their scarred skin and smoldering eyes, humans find them monstrous. When a hunter and a torch approach a *root*—someone who is magic but doesn't know it yet—the human will assume the torch is trying to hurt them, and the hunter trying to save them. Even when it's the other way around."

"That's why *you* came for me," I said, realization dawning. I wondered how I would have reacted if Eligor came for me first, his red-hot eyes glowing from the darkness. Sitri, on the other hand, looked human. Movie-star handsome, maybe, but not supernaturally distinct.

I looked again at the torches we passed. I'd gotten used to their appearance, but that didn't make them less startling. We hadn't seen many on the way down, but now they were on both sides of the path. Almost like they were *lining up* for us. I noticed several of them were staring at me. When I met their eyes, they gave me a slight nod. Almost a subtle bow.

"It's because of what happened," Sitri whispered to me. "They're kind of in awe of you."

"Of me? Why?" I picked up the pace, taking larger strides forward. Being underground was creeping me out. I needed to get outside.

"Hunters don't fall very often. And never like *that*. Almost everyone here fell at the same time, when Zeus ordered them to kill his own family. Their faith stemmed from the belief that he was *good*. When his commands went against their conscience, they shorted out. But a few fall gradually. Some spend too much time with humans, or read too much literature, listen to the wrong conversations, or even enjoy music or food too much. It only takes a moment. A sudden realization, the smallest doubt. Some fall for love. They start families, and live a human life for a while… until they watch everyone they know grow old and die."

"Hunters were formed to live forever—even without Zeus's energy they hardly age. Eventually, when they've exhausted all human experiences, many make their way here and devote themselves to service, just for a sense of purpose."

"Others give in to guilt, regret and despair. They refuse to serve any new master, and instead become desperados. Vigilantes. Hunting out what they consider to be evil, trying to get Zeus to forgive them and take them back. They continue the mission, unguided, unaided, hoping for redemption. Hunting out all magical creatures and killing them, because it was the last command they were given by their master. They take a finger as proof of their kill, and have necklaces full of the rotting bones of their victims."

"That's awful," I said.

"It gets worse. Once close to a source of magic, many find the temptation too strong to resist, and take the magic for themselves."

"Is that possible? How?"

"They eat their victims. Since hunters were made to be mirrors of Zeus's power, they are unique in being able to store and channel the energy of other beings. Torches that continue to hunt are called reapers. But if they start eating their kills, we call them leeches. Feeding on their kills makes them stronger, but also warps their minds and bodies. They become monstrous. Deformed and hungry for more power. Some have been around for a long time, and are very powerful. These are what humans might call demons. Most supernatural creatures that humans fear are based on leech sightings... seeing them kill and eat their victims, sucking out the blood, gnawing on bones."

We finally reached the mouth of the cave and emerged into the light, but I shuddered despite myself.

"Is that what will happen to Puriel?" I asked.

"Your hunter buddy?" Sitri said, shooting me a dark look. "That depends."

"On what?"

"Whether Able lets him live that long."

We went back inside and I followed Sitri to another room on the second floor that I somehow hadn't discovered yet. The ceiling was high and the room was so wide it looked like a hotel lobby. I counted five dark leather couches, each with a coffee table and several comfortable looking armchairs. A handful of round tables were scattered throughout the room as well. The ceiling and far wall were inset with mirrors, which made the room seem twice as large. Bright light streamed in through the large windows, which looked out over the amphitheater. I wondered if I'd had an audience during my fight with Mist, and if so, who was watching.

A long table was up against the wall, filled with silver trays full of snacks and cookies, mugs, sparkling water, and tea and coffee in large hot water containers. Sitri poured himself a cup of coffee and I made some tea and piled up cookies on to a small dish. I felt uncomfortable with the idea of Puriel being put to death, but I didn't want to bring it up in case it sounded like I was defending him. It was touching that Sitri cared so much about how the torches were treated, and I understood it—especially when he'd been living with Mist and the others who treated them like second class citizens. But I was still annoyed that he'd assumed the worst about me. At the same time, something still felt off about Nevah. Even this huge, empty room felt weird. Like it was built to be seen, but not used. Deceptive somehow. I didn't want Sitri to think I was ungrateful, but I did want him to understand how I was feeling.

"Okay," I said. "I get it. Looks can be deceiving, right? But it's more than just that. Why does everyone here use different names? Why does it feel like everybody has been lying to me. *Hiding* from me? And come on, we're basically talking about angels and demons here, right? Don't you ever worry that we're on the wrong side of things?"

"Good and evil is just propaganda, don't you see that? Those torches fought for you. *Died* for you."

"I didn't ask them too!"

"But it should have at least made it clear who is on your side, and who is trying to kill you."

"It did. I get that part. Hunters are dangerous. But in a war, both sides believe they are the heroes. And the hunters are just following orders, doing what they think is right—just like the torches. Are they even responsible for what they do?"

Sitri's eyes were wide and he was looking at me in disbelief. I realized I sounded crazy, defending his sworn enemies. Enemies who had *just* tried to kill me, and killed several torches in the process. I was basically confirming his fears about me. But I wasn't really thinking about all the hunters. I was just thinking about one. The one in the cell in the basement. Broken and miserable. Because of me. All of my arguments were really a thinly-veiled defense of Puriel, and I didn't even know why I cared so much.

Sitri looked disappointed with me.

"Do you really think Alice is evil? Sam? *Me*?"

I bit my lip. "No, not evil. Of course not. But maybe, both sides have been fighting so long, have lost so much, that neither side can see the other clearly anymore. And also… most of you are guests here, but Able calls the shots, right? He's Zeus's brother. I just wish I knew exactly what he wanted from me."

"I see," Sitri said, rubbing his jaw. "This is about Able. He can be intimidating, even scary. Especially now that you know who he really is. It's no wonder you're confused. Humans have always misunderstood him. You think my loyalty is misplaced, that I've been deceived. So let me tell you my story. I was one of the first that Zeus turned his back on. Without his presence, his light, I was nothing. I roamed the earth for centuries before Able took me in. Gave me a purpose again. A mission. When Zeus came for Able, I defended him. They fought, and Able had the upper hand. He might have defeated Zeus, except Zeus used his own son Hermes—Sam—as a human shield. Zeus traded Sam's life for his own freedom, and Able accepted. He chose to save his nephew, rather than land the finishing blow."

"Over the years I've watched Able open Nevah to thousands of refugees from around the world—Zeus's forgotten creatures and progeny, torches and human descendants from former deities, anyone or anything that was in danger from Zeus's magical genocide." Sitri drained his coffee and set down the cup with a clatter. His brow furled and I could see that he was getting worked up.

"And don't forget who Zeus chose to keep as his companions. Aphrodite was cast out and shamed, while Athena was kept. She's a vicious monster. All brain, no heart. Hera disowned Heph because of his 'deformity.' Zeus tried to get Athena to marry him but she refused, disgusted by him. Aphrodite agreed to marry him, even though she was in love with someone else, because otherwise he would have been thrown out of the family. And after all that, Zeus picked them, over everyone else."

"Why are you yelling at me?" I asked. Sitri's voice had been growing louder until it practically echoed in the cavernous room. "Besides I know this already. And I'm not saying Zeus isn't a major jerk. It's just—this is all really new to me, and I don't want to just blindly accept what people are telling me."

"Did you also know that Dion is Stephanie's son? Zeus was abusing her, even as a child, and got her pregnant. His own daughter. Able saved her, by removing her from Zeus's reach and bringing her into the underworld. After many centuries, they fell in love, united by their mission to save innocents."

This was new—and a little different from the story Stephanie told me. I wondered which was really true. I bit my lip but didn't say anything.

"If you already know all of this, and you still don't know which side you want to be on, maybe you should decide whether or not you really belong here."

Sitri said this quietly, but his words rang in my ears as he stormed out of the room. He was upset, obviously, but I don't think I'd done anything to deserve being treated like that. And I didn't *choose* to be here. Able said I was free to go, but also that I'd probably die out there on my own. Not much of a choice.

I felt like I'd pushed Sitri away from me. And for what—I'd never convince him to change his views. I just wished he could understand what I was feeling.

* * *

By the time I reached my room, I felt miserable. Sitri had been one of my closest friends here. And the way my pulse raced when I was around him, I can't say I wasn't hoping for something more. His loyalty was admirable, and I longed to have as much certainty. But I just didn't. Something about Nevah didn't feel right.

I jumped off my bed when someone knocked in the evening—I was hoping it was Sitri. My face fell when I discovered Alice instead. She was wearing a simple navy dress that looked classic, and holding a basket.

"I have something for you," she said. "I know it can get lonely in the house. We've lived together a long time; sometimes we go days without speaking. I thought you could use some company."

She reached into the basket and pulled out a kitten—the gray one with blue eyes, the same one Sitri had given me at JDRI. It seemed like ages ago now. At first I pulled back, remembering the vision I'd had last time. But he was so adorable. I checked to make sure my gloves were on before reaching out for him. I'd hardly thought of him since that first day, when I'd met Sitri and my whole life had changed. But I was glad to see he was alright. I wondered if Alice had sensed that I was having a bad day, or whether Sitri had asked her to deliver the kitten to cheer me up, as an indirect apology. But that was probably wishful thinking.

"Dinner's in twenty minutes," she said, coming into my room and rifling through my closet. She pulled out a black dress with a floral pattern stitched into the fabric and laid it across my bed. "I think this one would look amazing on you," she said, looking me over. I was wearing the same dark jeans I'd worn yesterday but they were dirty from my hike. Alice looked flawless by comparison, almost casually royal.

"Thanks," I said. "I'll meet you at dinner." I let the kitten down to explore the room and stripped off my dirty clothes. In the shower, I couldn't stop thinking about the graphic death I'd witnessed last time. Was this kitten still in danger? If he was, maybe I was too? I came out of the shower with a towel wrapped around me. When the kitten approached me and rubbed up against my bare leg, I flinched, but didn't pull away. I was afraid I'd see the same vision, but didn't. I only saw a gray fog, an emptiness. I breathed a sigh of relief.

Not every death is violent. It's only the sudden and tragic ones that I pictured so vividly. That I *experienced.* But that meant that, like Matt, this kitten's fate had been changed. It was more confirmation that my visions weren't set in stone, that the future was flexible. Despite the argument I'd had with Sitri, I felt a burst of optimism.

"I'm going to call you Ghost," I said, picking him up with my bare hands. It felt good to be so close to something warm and living. I didn't realize how starved I was for physical contact.

Ghost seemed to feel the same way; he purred and snuggled up against me. Then I set him down again and got ready for dinner.

The black dress hugged my body. I was self-conscious, but also impressed by my reflection in the mirror. The soft fabric felt smooth and cool against my skin. I was sure I'd never worn anything as expensive as this. With the black gloves up to my elbows, I looked like a movie star from another age. I noticed for the first time that my appearance had changed slightly—my skin looked smoother, and seemed to glow. My eyes, which had always been striking, now seemed unnaturally green, almost iridescent, like shallow water in a mountain lake. My hair was darker and shone with luxurious curls that spiraled down to my shoulders. I hardly recognized myself. I'd felt out of place in this house full of gods and goddesses, but I realized now I was starting to look more like them. Maybe it was a benefit of being surrounded by this much power and energy.

The only thing out of place was the block of colored legos around my neck. In the desk drawer I found a dozen expensive looking necklaces that sparkled with gold and gemstones. I reached instead for a simple, elegant strand of pearls. It was cold against my bare collarbone. It completed my outfit perfectly, but at the last minute I put it back and grabbed my chunk of legos instead. I wasn't going to change who I was for their approval.

I didn't understand why we had formal dinners anyway. There was always plenty of food in the kitchen. Sitri usually just made his own dinner and ate in one of the reading rooms, or sometimes outside to watch the sunset. That sounded a lot better to me than sitting through another stuffy dinner. Besides, as Mist kept bringing up, I wasn't family.

Everyone was already seated when I walked in. Dion's eyes travelled down my body, and his smirk made my skin glow. He jumped up and pulled a chair out for me. When I sat down, he whispered "You look ravishing." Even though I'd never go for a guy like him, it was nice to be appreciated—especially in the same room with Tori. At a table full of girls that could all have been supermodels, it was easy to feel inadequate.

Tonight I almost felt I could hold my own. Or at least that I wasn't the ugly duckling.

The table was unusually quiet. Everyone seemed preoccupied with their food. I realized I hadn't talked to most of the family since what happened yesterday, when I did the exact thing Stephanie had warned me against in our last conversation. While the heirs and torches seemed impressed by me, the immortals were basically pretending I didn't exist. At least Mist was keeping her mouth shut. After Sitri's meltdown, I didn't think I could handle anyone else yelling at me today.

To fill the silence, I tried to keep track of how everyone was related. I wondered who was the most powerful. Artemis, Persephone, Dionysus, Aphrodite, Hermes and Hephasteus were all half-siblings. Zeus was their father, and he'd abandoned them. More than that—he'd betrayed them. And killed people they loved. Maybe Sitri had a point. These weren't the bad guys.

Through the ceiling I could hear pounding noises, and realized it was probably torches repairing the hole in the roof. Somehow it made the silence even more awkward. I refilled my glass of wine from the bottle on the table just as dessert was brought out—raspberry sorbet with flakes of white chocolate. As if on signal, Able tapped his glass to get our attention, even though nobody was talking.

"Yesterday's events were surprising, but we've learned two things," Able said. "One, Kaidance accurately foretold an attack on Nevah that we did not expect. We didn't handle it well. They should never have gotten into the house. And to get that near to the accomplishing their mission—that was inexcusable. Heph and I will be working on new defenses to make sure this doesn't happen again."

"And the second thing?" Sam asked.

"Kaidance is more powerful than we thought," Able said, looking directly at me.

"From what I heard, she didn't really *do* anything." Mist cut in, rolling her eyes. "Besides nearly throwing her life away and ruining everything."

"I agree, Kaidance was reckless. But she's young, and it's our responsibility to take care of her. The power I was referring to, however, is the power to change fate. She had a vision of Matt being killed by the hunter, but she stopped it from happening. Now Matt's recovering."

"You want to use her gift for battles," Stephanie guessed, eyeing her husband critically. "Giving the soldiers foresight, in order to avoid their deaths."

"Possibly," Able said, folding his fingers together.

"That's not what we discussed," Stephanie said, pursing her lips.

"It's all we have at the moment. Maybe with more training she'll be able to unlock more abilities. But for now, we'll use any advantage she can give us."

"Maybe you should ask her first," Alice said quietly. Heads turned toward me. Sitri said I needed to decide whether I wanted to be here, but he didn't say I'd have to decide today. Was I really going to help Able wage his war against Zeus? I still didn't trust him, but I did trust Sitri. I was pretty sure he wouldn't intentionally hurt me. And I considered Sam, Heph and Alice as friends, even though I hadn't known them long. If I was forced to pick sides, I'd choose this one. But I also wanted to know what I was getting into.

"What exactly are you asking me to do?" I asked, putting down my fork and holding Able's gaze. "I can accept that Zeus is a jerk. He did try to kill me after all. If you want me to help you defend Nevah, I can do that. But it sounds like you're hoping for something else. Something more."

Able swirled the wine in his cup and chose his words carefully. His gold rings sparkled.

"The truth is, we've been at a stalemate for thousands of years—ever since the Fates hid the golden shears. We can slow down Zeus's purge, by trying to save a few of the heirs before the hunters get to them, but we can't stop him. If you can see the threads of life, however, you must have some connection to the Fates. Maybe you can discover where they are or where they hid the shears. Maybe you can get them back."

"And if I do?" I asked.

"Then you can cut Zeus's thread," Stephanie interrupted, her eyes gleaming. Her youthful beauty contrasted with the terrifying look in her eyes. "End all of this. The tyranny, the bloodshed."

I looked at Alice, then at Sam. Neither of them flinched at Stephanie's words. Which meant, this is what they all wanted from me. What they expected me to do. *Puriel was right.* They want me to become a *deicidium*—a godkiller.

I told Able I'd do whatever I could to help, without explicitly agreeing to murder anybody. Then I excused myself for the night. A lot of conditions had to be met before any of this mattered anyway. Finding the shears, figuring out how to use them... maybe we'd never even get to that point. For now, I'd stay and train, and help defend my new friends and Nevah however I could. With that decision made, I felt calmer than I had since arriving, and fell asleep with Ghost curling up next to me in bed.

I woke up hours later to scratches on the door. I checked the clock next to my bed—it was past three in the morning. The room was nearly pitch black but I could see Ghost's light-colored body at the door, trying to push it open with his tiny paws.

"What is it?" I asked. After dinner, Sam had dropped off a sandbox in the corner of my room for Ghost to use, and I'd already given him some scraps of food.

"What do you want?" I asked again. I picked him up and tried to calm him down, but he squirmed away from me and went back to the door. I was curious—what was he after?

When I opened the door, Ghost scampered down the hall. At first I thought he just wanted to stretch his legs, but his path was direct and straight. I followed behind him quietly. My heart raced as we started descending. Towards the dungeon. Towards Puriel. I sighed in relief when he turned left and went in a different direction. When he reached a closed door at the end of a hall, he waited and looked back at me.

I pushed the door open and held my nose. It smelled in here. *Like blood.* There was a wide wooden table in the center of the room, and gleaming utensils hanging on the wall. Large knives, saws and other items I couldn't identify—a butchery, I guessed. For a house this large, and this isolated, it would make sense to butcher their own meat. It would be easy for Mist to bring down wild boar or deer.

But then I heard movement and turned around. My eyes widened when I saw the cages. There were some live chickens, but it was the cage full of kittens that drew my eye. Some looked like Ghost, and I wondered if he had family in there.

What were they doing down here, in a room like this? I looked again at the sharp blades hanging on the wall, gleaming in the darkness. My skin crawled as I tried to imagine what they could be used for. That's when I saw the hammer. The same hammer I'd seen in my vision.

No.

My blood ran cold and I shivered. I picked Ghost up and squeezed him to my chest protectively. Somehow he'd avoided the fate I'd seen for him, but apparently he wasn't the only one I needed to worry about.

I reached out with trembling fingers and touched one of the other kittens in the cage. I pulled my hand away like I'd been burned. My eyes started watering as I touched another kitten, and another.

It was all the same. Every single one met the same horrible death. Their tiny skulls crushed by a hammer. Probably in this very room. Held down by a pair of strong hands.

As I touched the kittens, I realized my visions were getting clearer. Usually I jerked away immediately. I'd never really *tried* to see visions like this, through prolonged contact. But this time, I wanted to know more. If someone in this house, someone I was living with, could be this cruel, I wanted to know about it. I put Ghost down and picked up a small black kitten and concentrated. Even though seeing the mangled body on the table was horrifying—watching his tiny limbs spasm as he clung to the last seconds of life—I held on.

My stomach twisted and my eyes filled with tears, but the scene became clear in front of me. No longer a fragmented flash of the future, but a living scene, a loop playing on repeat. It was almost like I was there. Watching the hammer come down, the kitten squirming against those big strong hands. A flash of light caught my eye and

I focused in on the hands, which were sporting several sparkling, jeweled rings. One of them was engraved with symbols and had a black star sapphire, with six gleaming rays that slid across the surface.

18

I woke up suddenly, my heart pounding and my sheets damp from sweat. My fingers were wrapped tightly around my blankets. Last night I'd grabbed Ghost and returned to my room. I wore myself out, thinking in circles, until I fell into a dreamless sleep.

But now everything came flooding back.

So many kittens, all with the same horrible future. How long had Able been looking for me? How many times had he used this test on other heirs or roots, hoping to find someone who could help him defeat his brother? He'd been planning this for a long time, and he wasn't afraid to kill innocents to get what he wanted. *And now he had it.*

Ghost jumped on my stomach and stretched out. I stroked his soft fur absently, wondering how many kittens had been sacrificed for this one project. To find *me*. Hundreds? Thousands?

I shuddered at the thought of a kitten cemetery somewhere on the grounds, filled with a small mountain of tiny bodies. My stomach growled loudly and Ghost perked up, looking at me with surprise.

"Guess we better eat breakfast, huh? I'll bring you back something good." I put on a clean pair of jeans, a long sleeve shirt and my all-stars.

My adventures of last night seemed far away in the daytime. The house was as bright and luxurious as always. The dining room was filled with the scent of bacon, strong coffee and freshly baked bread.

I thought about grabbing food and returning to my room, but I wouldn't be able to avoid everyone from now on—they would know something was up. So I sat down and pretended that everything was fine.

I was halfway through breakfast when Sitri came in the room. He was wearing a dark shirt that clung to his chest and his skin was damp—like he'd been out running. He hadn't shaved in several days, and there were circles under his eyes like he hadn't been sleeping well. Even so, he looked amazing. His scent was so strong it seemed almost more delicious than the bacon.

"Hey," he said awkwardly, rubbing the back of his neck. My mouth was full of toast, so I just nodded to him. He piled his plate up with scrambled eggs and sat down next to me.

"Listen, I'm sorry about yesterday," he said. "I know you just got here, and this is all new to you. I can't expect you just to take our word for everything. You're right to be hesitant, to make sure you're on the right side of things. It just proves what a good person you are. I was mad yesterday, because the torches and Able try so hard to earn trust and loyalty, by doing good things, saving people, and almost everyone still treats them like villains. I've watched it happen, over and over again, for centuries. I was just hoping you'd be different."

I almost choked on my food. Somehow Sitri had a way of saying the nicest things, and then ruining it with something hurtful. I stared at him, but he didn't seem to notice that he'd said anything wrong. I wanted to defend myself, or say that I *was* different. I wanted to tell him what I'd seen last night—but I knew he would just defend Able.

Sitri was too loyal to see the truth: Able wasn't doing all this out of the goodness of his heart. Saving heirs and roots. He was building an army. A perimeter defense. And *weapons*. If Stephanie was right, I was the most powerful weapon of all, in Able's hands. The only thing that could kill Zeus.

That's when I realized I had to leave. If I stayed here, Able wouldn't stop until he found his golden shears, and then he'd try to make them use them. On the most powerful of the Olympians... a god who has been alive for thousands of years. *Me*.

For most of my life people have seen me as a killer. And I've tried to prove them wrong. I tried to show I was normal. Nice. Or at the very least, not homicidal. Able wanted to reverse all that, and turn me into the one thing I swore I'd never become.

And it seemed like neither Zeus nor Able cared who got hurt in their quest for victory. Able may not be the devil, but who's to say if we defeated Zeus, Able wouldn't become just as bad? Or Worse?

But I couldn't expect Sitri to understand that. Besides, I didn't have to leave right away. I should stay longer, keep training, and work with Stephanie to unlock my powers. Maybe until I was strong enough to defend myself. Then at least I'd have a chance of surviving on my own, and protecting those I cared about.

"I'm going to the armory," I said suddenly. "To train. Want to come?"

Sitri raised an eyebrow at me and the side of his lip curved into a smile.

"I'd love to, but I've got some things I need to help Able with. I'll see if one of the torches is available, or send Sam down if I see him. Heph is probably down in the forge already. He can set you up with some practice dummies."

I stopped in my room to give Ghost some bacon. My eyes fell on the bag with the sawed-off shotgun and my sword. I'd brought it back with me after the attack. I thought about returning it, but decided to leave it in my room. It was nice to know I had weapons available if I needed them. And it's not like they would miss them, with the hundreds of items in the armory.

I found Heph in the forge, sharpening a long, wicked looking axe. Sparks shot out around his body. He was framed by the orange glow of the forge and the bluish light coming in from the side door. I waited until he noticed me, then smiled when he looked up.

"What can I help you with?" he asked.

"Just wanted to play with some sharp objects," I said.

"We've got plenty of those," he said. "Take whatever you like."

"And maybe some help on how to use them?"

He set down the axe and pulled a shirt on.

"Sure. I can help for a while, until someone else shows up. I'm more of an artist than a fighter."

"Well, I'm basically useless, so I'm sure you're way ahead of me."

I picked out a short sword that was similar to the one in my room—not quite as pretty, nor as lightweight. But functional. My eye was also drawn to a small dagger with twin golden snakes spiraling down the handle. Rubies were used for the snakes' eyes. Not exactly practical, but walking around the house with a big sword at my side seemed silly. I could conceal this in my sleeve or tuck it into the back of my jeans.

"You want to start with that?" Heph said, nodding at the dagger.

"Don't you just... point and stab?" I asked, gesturing lamely in front of me.

He smiled and his eyes sparkled. He put down the sword he'd picked out and gestured towards the practice mat. I followed him.

"Keep the sheath on," he said, smirking. "I may heal quickly but I'm not fond of pain."

He showed me how to hold the knife, where the major arteries were, and how to deflect a punch so that the attacker exposed a vital organ.

"The problem with this is, hunters are way faster than you. And stronger. And they wear armor."

"So I'm screwed," I said.

"Not necessarily. Your best bet is the element of surprise. Take them down before they know you're a threat. Jab the blade up through their jaw, slash it across their neck, or drive it straight into their ear. Those will slow them down, and maybe give you a shot at running away. Or if you have a sword or the shotgun we gave you last time, you could blast their head off, or pierce their heart. It's not easy, with the armor, but if you get just the right angle, below their armpit, you can reach it."

"Great," I said, without enthusiasm. I couldn't see myself doing any of those things.

"Maybe we should work on defense instead." He took the dagger from me and taught me several ways to block a knife without injury and disarm an attacker. I doubt I could actually use them in a fight, but they were fun to learn.

"You try again. Attack me, then try to strike something critical."

I lunged at him, but he slapped my hand away every time I got near him. Soon my arms were red from all the times he'd hit me, and I hadn't landed a blow once. He wasn't moving quickly, he just seemed to easily shift his body weight away from my attacks. Half the time I stumbled forward from my own momentum.

"You're too direct," he said. It's obvious where you're headed. Your eyes give you away first, then your feet. Way before your hand ever gets close to me. You need to look like you're going to strike in one place, then change last minute and strike with another dagger."

"I don't have another dagger," I said.

"That's your main problem. Always have a backup weapon." He pulled a tiny device from his pocket. It looked like a keychain with a garage door opener attached. When he clicked the red button, the serpentine dagger ripped out of my hand and flew towards the wall. It stuck there, halfway up the wall, held by some invisible force.

"What the hell was that?" I asked, rubbing my palm.

"A powerful electro-magnet," Heph smiled. "I put it up once because Tori was always complaining about how weak I was, and that I needed to learn to fight. She got the point. Why fight when you can just disarm your enemies? Why risk your life when you can build an army of robots to do it for you?"

"You have an army of robots?" I asked, my eyes wide.

"I *could* have one," he said. "The point is, always use the right tool for the job. Archimedes said, 'Give me a lever long enough and a fulcrum on which to place it, and I shall move the world.' Basically, find the right tool and the right place to apply pressure, and there's nothing you can't do."

"Still cheating, I see." Matt was crossing the armory with a smug smile.

"It's *not* cheating," Heph said with a frown. "It's called using your brain. You might still have one if you stopped ramming your head into things."

"Whatever. A giant magnet to disarm your opponent? It's sneaky."

"It's effective. Would you rather fight fairly and die with honor?"

"Absolutely," Matt said with a wide grin.

"Great. You can teach her then. Teach her how to overwhelm an enemy with brute force. See how well that works for her. I've got work to do."

"Hold up, I was just teasing. Plus I need your help with something." Matt held up a gold nugget as big as my thumb. "Got this from a torch in exchange for some chocolate cake. Seems like not all of them are as tough as they pretend to be. Think you can turn it into a ring?"

Heph took the nugget and squinted at it.

"Sure, what size?"

Matt looked at his fingers for a minute, then grabbed my hand and held it out. "About this size," he said, pointing to my ring finger.

"Wait, is this for Priya?" I asked. Heph raised his eyebrows and smiled.

"Wow man, about time. Congratulations."

"I know, right?" Matt grinned. "I just—after what happened… life's short, you know?"

"I've got some spare diamonds in the back," Heph said. "Took them out of some broken swords I recycled. Four carats should be big enough?"

My mouth dropped open. "Um, I don't know Priya that well, but personally I wouldn't want a rock that big on my finger."

"What would you get?" Matt asked.

"Something understated. Classic. A simple gold band with one or two carats. Probably set in the band, rather than a solitaire—otherwise it would get caught in everything."

"Were you a jeweler or something?" Heph asked. I shrugged. No need to tell them that Jessie and I spent weeks planning our weddings when we were twelve, after we found a catalogue of engagement rings in the trash bin.

We headed back into the forge. Heph moved the axe out of the way and brought out smaller tools to work on the ring.

"What's that for?" Matt asked, nodding at the axe.

"The hunter they caught," Heph said. "He's being executed tomorrow."

* * *

I practically raced down the stairs to the cellar. This time, there were two torches outside. I wondered if they were the same ones who were outside my room earlier, then felt bad that I couldn't tell them apart. But that didn't matter right now. I knew Able and Sitri wouldn't want me talking to Puriel again, but I couldn't stay away. I had to see him.

"Let me talk to him," I demanded, when the torches crossed their dark swords in front of the door. "Please," I said. "One last time." One of them put away his sword, and the other followed. I was a little surprised they listened to me. I wondered if it was a courtesy to me—or Puriel.

I gasped when I entered the room. Puriel looked like shit. His whole body was bruised, and he was bleeding from several deep cuts that looked like they'd been made with precision. His lip was split and he had a black eye.

"It's interesting…" he said, raising his head slowly.

"What is?" I asked.

"Pain. I've never really felt it before. I don't think I've ever really been injured before—with

Deus by my side, skin, flesh and bone were just resources. Cut them out, and they'd regenerate. These wounds…" He reached down and put his finger in one of the cuts. "Just sitting there. Oozing blood. It makes me feel… limited. Finite."

"I am sorry," I said.

"At least it will be over tomorrow," he said.

"You've heard then?"

"The torches outside told me. It was kind of them. I always saw them as traitors and fools, and now I'm one of them. Death will be a relief."

I frowned. I didn't like seeing him like this. I'm glad he was calm about it, but I hated that he was so miserable he'd prefer death to sticking around.

"Being a torch isn't that bad," I said. "Some torches get married. Raise children. Fight for a cause."

"Worthless attempts to fill the gaping holes in their hearts left by Deus's omnipotence."

"He's not exactly *all-powerful*," I said, frowning. "I mean, he sent you here to kill me, right? And you failed."

"Do you think Deus hasn't thought of this? Hasn't accounted for everything?"

"Don't tell me you *meant* to fall."

"Of course not," Puriel said bitterly. "I had no idea what was going to happen. But that doesn't mean he didn't. Actually he sent us to capture you. That was the mission. But in that moment, when you appeared in front of me out of nowhere, willing to die for that heir—his command was to kill. And I didn't strike."

He hung his head sadly. I didn't know what to say, so I moved closer to him and put my hand on his arm. He looked up at me in surprise.

"You don't belong here, you know. With them. You're different. It almost makes me think that I was right to hesitate. Maybe Deus meant for me to refuse. Maybe he still has plans for you. And if that's what he wants, maybe I served him after all."

He sounded hopeful, but I could tell he didn't really believe it. I turned to leave. I didn't say anything. What could I say? *See you later?* We both knew there would be no later. Not for him.

I was halfway out the door when I heard him mutter, "I'm sorry about your friends." He said it so quietly I almost didn't hear him. I turned back and stared at him.

"Which friends?" I asked cautiously.

"The other girls, from the institution where I found you."

"What are you talking about?" I asked, my heart pounding in my chest. Puriel raised his eyebrows, but then confusion gave way to understanding and he shook his head.

"I assumed they would have told you. But now I can see that they haven't. If this plan failed, which it did, we were supposed to regroup and meet back where I first found you. For your friends."

"Jessie and Sarah? But why?"

"For leverage. For bait. I don't know exactly, those were the orders. Get you, or get your friends."

I clenched my fists so hard my fingernails dug into my palms.

"And you told Able this?"

"He can be very persuasive."

"I *have* to save them." I said.

"They've probably been taken already."

I practically ran up the stairs. At first I was heading to confront Able, but changed my mind and went straight to my room to calm down. I felt like the sky had fallen. I was furious at Able for not telling me my friends were in danger, but challenging him now wouldn't help. He'd probably decided my friends weren't worth saving, that I was more important, and that if I knew the truth I would try to leave. I wondered if Sitri and him had discussed this together, and whether Sitri had argued at first, but ultimately agreed with Able. Like he always does. He hadn't told me about Puriel's execution this morning; maybe he was keeping this from me as well. I'd been hanging on to the slim hope that maybe he'd be on *my* side, that he'd choose me—but that was ridiculous. He'd just met me, and he'd been working for Able for millenia.

I'd already decided to leave, but I thought I had more time. I wasn't ready to go out on my own, but I didn't have a choice. If Sarah and Jessie were in danger, I needed to save them. I wasn't going to beg or ask permission—I was leaving, no matter what.

Able and Sitri said I was free to leave, but I'm pretty sure if I asked, they'd try and talk me out of it. Based on how methodically Able had been searching for me, it didn't seem like he was just going to let me go. And of course if he really wanted to keep me here, he could just throw me in Puriel's cell after they killed him.

I didn't think Sitri would let him do that, but I also knew if I told him I was leaving, he'd run to Able. Which meant I had to leave on my own. The problem was, if I *did* run into a bunch of hunters trying to kidnap Sarah and Jesse, I couldn't really do anything to stop them. What happened with Puriel was a fluke—I couldn't count on it to happen again. I needed a guardian. But all of the torches here were too loyal to Able... except one. I could only think of one idea, but it was a bad one.

I must be crazy.

But I packed anyway. I grabbed a backpack and stuffed it with some practical clothes. I also dumped out the jewelry drawer and filled my pockets with expensive-looking necklaces. I could pawn them later. I didn't exactly have a plan, other than to grab Jessie and Sarah and run off to Bermuda or something. Why not?

I'd kept the golden dagger with the twin snakes after leaving the armory, and tucked it into the back of my jeans. I also grabbed the bag with the shotgun and shells, and the sword Sitri had picked out for me.

Then I left a note for Sitri in the bathroom.

It's too much. I don't want to hurt anyone. I thought for a minute, about what I was about to do, and wrote: *And I don't want anyone to hurt, because of me.*

I left Ghost in a basket outside the infirmary with a note for Alice to take care of him, and snuck into the kitchen for some granola bars. I wished I could take Hades' invisibility cap but I didn't dare sneak into his office.

Then I crept back to Puriel's cell downstairs. This time it was unguarded. I grabbed the large iron skeleton keys and opened the door to the cell. Puriel looked up at me, his eyes cautiously curious, but he didn't say anything when I held my finger to my lips. I crept closer to him and whispered.

"Did you mean what you said earlier? You don't regret what happened?"

"I don't think I said I don't *regret* it..."

"Whatever, I mean—can I unlock these cuffs or are you going to strangle me with your chains?"

He looked confused, then his eyes widened.

"You want to let me go? Go *where*? I have no home, no purpose, no friends. Where would I go?"

"But they'll kill you."

"What do I have to live for? I failed to serve him with my life. It would have been glorious to die in battle for his service."

"Listen carefully. I *forbid* you to die. I don't want to listen to your pity party right now, and if that seems insensitive, it's because the only two people I care about in the world might be in danger. From *your* former comrades. I should just leave you in here, except... I can't just let them kill you. Plus everyone keeps telling me that if I go out there on my own, I'm pretty much dead meat."

"You want *me* to go with *you,*" he said slowly. He was obviously questioning my sanity. I thought I even saw the corner of his lip turn up in a smirk.

"I get it. Stupidest idea ever. I thought if I let you go, you'd be grateful or something. But forget it."

I turned to leave, then said over my shoulder, "have fun at your execution."

"Wait." He said it quietly, but with decision. He held his wrists out to me.

This time it was my turn to hesitate.

"I promise I won't kill you, okay?"

"You don't want to redeem yourself to Zeus?"

"I've been around a long time. I've never seen a torch get *redeemed*. It's an urban legend, a fairy tale torches tell their human children. To try and explain why they should *be good*, when their own fathers had fallen. Some torches live remarkably noble lives, trying to find meaning in kindness and generosity. Others indulge in more carnal pleasures, hoping to feel anything other than the constant shame and bitterness of being cast out. Most live long enough to spend centuries doing both. But it doesn't matter. Once they're gone, Deus doesn't notice them at all. He's blind to them, and all their striving, and efforts to please him. Seraphim joke that wanting to be *redeemed* is the torch's curse. It causes them to become reapers. Which is a nice thought. I mean, even if Deus doesn't notice, they're still doing our job for us. Only one problem: seraphim weren't built to be alone. When we hunt, we hunt in packs. We give our prey a clean death. And even when the kill is hard, we know that we are right. Because we are doing Deus's will. And because we're doing it together. But reapers hunt alone. They have doubts, and fears. They don't know if killing magical creatures without Deus's command is justified. Plus, the glow of magic is similar to Zeus's power. Seraphim don't need it, we have an inexhaustible supply of energy. But when we lose it… it's like our heart has been torn out. We have an aching hole inside, hungry to be filled. We were built that way, to be dependent on an external source of energy."

"Few reapers can resist feeding, and becoming leeches. Disgusting. Reprehensible. They lose all sense and reason. They grow black and vile, crusted over with the blood of their victims."

"So you see, even though I can't sense much magic coming from you right now, I couldn't be sure there wouldn't be more of it. And I couldn't be sure that I'd be able to resist it, and turn into the thing that is every seraphim's worst fear. A fate much worse than the death that awaits me tomorrow."

I blinked and shook my head. I still didn't know if he'd help me, but I was pretty sure he wouldn't kill me. Plus what choice did I have?

"I'm convinced," I said, unlocking his restraints. Puriel's sword was on a table outside the cell. I wondered why it hadn't been taken to the armory yet. He reached for it slowly, then grabbed the handle and lifted it up. The silver gleam on the sword's edge told me it was razor sharp, but it didn't glow with fire like it had before.

"It's heavy," Puriel said, half to himself. "It always felt light to me before, as easy as raising my arm. Now I can hardly swing it." Puriel's white shirt was soiled from his time in the cell. I look around for his armor but couldn't see it.

"It's better than nothing," I said. "You're lucky they left it down here. Maybe they were planning on using it on you tomorrow. Can we go now?"

I found a door that led outside and we crept across the grass in the shadows. To our left, a large bonfire was burning, surrounded by silhouetted figures. Two of them were swinging a large bundle into the flames.

"They're burning the bodies," Puriel said. "The fallen seraphim."

"At least they're distracted," I said, keeping my eyes forward. As we neared the edge of the property, I started to feel good about my decision. This was the right choice. I don't want to be a pawn in some supernatural war. Even if I do nothing, by being at Nevah I put everyone at risk. Without me, it would go back to being a stalemate, a cold war. Hunters, reapers and leeches, killing heirs and roots. A whole supernatural world I knew nothing about. A world I was deliberately turning my back on. Once I got Jesse and Sarah back, Puriel could go his way and I'd go mine. We'd hide out somewhere. We'd get fake identities. We'd have a normal, human life. Maybe learn to surf. Zeus and Able could keep fighting for another thousand years.

I breathed a sigh of relief when we crossed the park and entered into the trees at the edge of the property. I thought Able would have a perimeter detail up or something. Or Heph would have picked us up on his high-tech surveillance systems. But maybe we were unremarkable—they were looking for magical beings, full of energy. We were just two shadows in the dark, without much of our own magic. Through the trees and the mist, I caught a glimpse of the road up ahead. We were going to make it. That's when I heard the roar behind us.

Puriel whirled around and pulled out his sword as a dark figure tackled him to the ground. I heard a yell, and the sound of blows being landed. Then there was a slicing, gushing sound. I cried out, grabbing at the dark shape and rolling him off Puriel. My face lit up with relief when I saw that he was breathing. The sword had gotten pinned on the ground behind him when he fell, plunging into the body of the attacker. He was large, with some kind of horned helmet… but one horn had been broken off.

"*No!*" I cried, leaning over the dark shape. I turned his head into the light so I could see his face, and I choked back a sob when Matt's features were visible. Blood bubbled up from his lips. My vision clouded with tears, but I still recognized the familiarity of the scene. Matt on the grassy soil, his blood spreading out like a cape beneath him. The gleaming sword in his chest, with its golden handle, the glittering blue gemstones, the symbol of a crown. Outside, at night. Just like my vision.

I felt dizzy and gulped down air. I tried to stand up, my arms reaching out for balance, but my knees buckled and I fell to the ground next to the body, sobbing into his chest. I hadn't saved Matt at all. I'd ensured his death. I was exactly the monster everyone thought I was.

I appreciate you…

Thanks for reading *The Scarlet Thread!* I'm working on book two (*The Golden Scissors)* and it should be ready by March 1st, 2017.

You can preorder it now, or sign up on my email list and I'll let you know when it's ready. In the meantime, I've started several other young adult series I think you'll enjoy. You can get part one of *Orpheum*, *Shearwater* and *Prescient* for free if you sign up on my website:

>> Sign up at UrbanEpics.com <<

Please leave a review of Scarlet Thread on Amazon right now, while the book is still fresh in your mind. Just a quick note on what you liked about the book—it'll just take a second and I'll appreciate it forever.

Click here to leave a review on Amazon.

Keep Reading

I'm adding the first four chapters of *Prescient* here in case you need something else to read *right now*. It's a time travel dystopia based on mythology and the Delphic Oracle. If you like it, you can get the first half for free (11 more chapters).

1

"How'd you ever talk me into this?" I muttered from the passenger seat of Crys's mom's Ford Aerostar, a green van she'd finally gotten access to when she passed her driver's license test a few weeks ago. Butterflies gnawed at my stomach as she pulled up to the curb and turned off the engine.

"Are you crazy? A party at Brett Peters' house? You know what I had to do to get us invited?" She flicked back her dark, curly hair, and checked her eyeliner in the rearview mirror.

I didn't know, but I could imagine. Crys had always been the more experienced between us.

This year she was dating Cody Myers, a hot senior on the soccer team.

Crys and I had been inseparable since third grade, so I was considered cool by association, kind of, in that most of the popular seniors tolerated my sophomoric presence. At least when Crys was around—she knew how to flirt and keep a conversation flying. Ten seconds around me and conversation would usually dry up. Crys said I was like a stone. With moss on it.

"There will probably be alcohol at this party," Crys said. "You don't have to have any. But if you do, drink slowly," she glared at me meaningfully.

"I'm never going to live this down, am I?" I said. Crys had stolen some vodka from her dad's liquor cabinet for her birthday, and we stayed in and made screwdrivers. It was fun until I threw up all over her mom's azaleas.

"At least I made it outside," I crossed my arms.

"I don't want to have to babysit you or take you home early. Stay sharp, stay in control. But also, loosen up. Have fun. You need a boyfriend, so we can double-date." Crys had been saying that for years. She'd had a boyfriend since I met her in 2nd grade. She'd gone through dozens of them since, but she always seemed to be in a relationship. Unlike me, who was perpetually single.

I could see Brett's house down the street. Not that I knew what his house looks like. Because I've never, like, crept around outside like a stalker. I swear. I'd been to parties before, but mostly lame ones, with cake and Doritos and Coke, where we watched movies or played board games. Last year there had even been a party where the parents weren't home, and we played spin the bottle. I made out with three different boys—the extent of my interaction with the opposite sex. But I didn't like any of them, so I'd just viewed it as practice.

Practice for Brett Peters.

And now I was opening the sliding door, getting out of the van, smoothing down my sweater and my straight blond hair, and turning red like an apple, something I always did when I was terrified. I'd had a crush on Brett since sixth grade. Then he'd moved up to High School and left me behind—not that he had any idea who I was.

Now I was a sophomore. He was a senior and next year he'd be going off to college. That meant, if we had any chance of being together, it had to happen this year. At least that's the argument Crys used when she was talking me into this party, even though we'd be two years younger than everyone else.

"You sure he won't mind me crashing?" I whispered. I tugged at the sleeves of my sweater, something I did when I was nervous. Somehow covering more skin made me feel less vulnerable.

"Cody said it was cool," Crys said.

"Cool if you could bring *me?*" I said. "Did you ask him if *Alicia* could come, or if you could bring a friend?" My heart pounded as Crys knocked on the door. Brett opened the door, wearing jeans and a flannel shirt.

"Hey guys," he said, looking right at me and smiling. He had perfect, tan skin, olive green eyes, and golden hair that always looked carefully sculpted in place. His smile was both charming and authentic. He looked like an old fashioned gentleman, but with a hint of a smirk that said he was no angel.

He gestured us inside but my knees felt wobbly so I hesitated. Crys gave me a shove and I stumbled inside. The house was trying to go for "rustic charm" and had been built to look sort of farmish on the inside and out, but the high ceilings and polished gleam on everything suggested wealth. That wasn't a surprise, everybody knew that Brett's dad had some kind of corporate job.

That's one of the things I always liked about Brett—he didn't flaunt his money and he wasn't a jerk to poorer students the way some rich kids were. He was just himself, and he got along with everybody. You couldn't help like him after having a conversation with him—even the teachers adored him. Or so I'd gathered, listening to other girls swoon over him in the restrooms at school. He hadn't said so much as "hi" to me personally. But that didn't mean I didn't know him.

I followed Crys inside towards the music and voices. There were at least twenty kids in the living room, and more in the kitchen and outside on the patio. There was a pool out back and some people were swimming. We grabbed a hard apple cider and some popcorn and found a place to sit for a while. Then Cody came by and whispered something to Crys.

"I'll be back in a little while, okay?" she said, squeezing my hand. Then she ditched me like a third wheel.

An hour later, I was still alone. Well, kind of alone. A senior named Dave had been talking to me for thirty minutes, asking me questions about drama, history, books. David's eyebrows looked like a long fuzzy caterpillar. I gave terse answers and avoided eye contact, my arms crossed in front of me as I leaned against the wall. I was hoping he'd get the hint and leave me alone, but he kept at it. Sometimes he would tease or make jokes, and I smiled politely, but with that edge that says *I'm listening to you, but I'm not enjoying myself.*

Part of me was pissed at Crys for dragging me to a party and then abandoning me. My eyes kept looking for Brett but I hadn't seen him in a long time. And then I'd feel bad for a moment, because I wasn't more friendly or because I should let Crys have a good time. *Why couldn't I just relax and enjoy myself?* I took a long sip of my cider.

"So what do your parents do?" Dave asked, trying to breathe life into the failing conversation.

"My mom died when I was nine," I said.

"Oh that... sucks," he said.

I didn't wait for the next question, which experience had told me would inevitably be "*how did she die?*" Not exactly small talk. Dave was confusing intimate conversation with intimacy, and probably thought if he got me to open up to him, he'd have a better shot of getting into my pants.

That was unfair, I censored myself. I try not to prejudge or assume things about people. I stop myself if I can, though I find myself doing it a lot. But then Dave proved my first guess right. He leaned in to kiss me, somehow thinking my vulnerability gave him permission. I stumbled backwards, crashing against the wall and spilling cider all over myself. *Awesome.*

"Excuse me," I pushed past him, "I have to go to the bathroom."

Once free I headed upstairs as if I knew where I was going. I needed some breathing space. I found the bathroom and tried to wash off the cider. I dried my clothes with toilet paper. The sweater was fine, but there were big wet spots on my jeans now. It looked like I'd peed my pants. I tied my sweater around my waist and checked myself out in the mirror. Mascara brings out my big round eyes, which sometimes hide behind the tips of my bangs. But other than that I'm pretty plain: my skin is pale and pasty, my face is a little too squarish, instead of the slim and smooth oval shape that models always have. And my mouth is too small for my face. Other than that, I'm not bad looking. Under the sweater I was wearing a tight green rock t-shirt, hip-hugging jeans that flared a little at the bottom, and a pair of black Converse all stars.

I stalled, not at all eager to rejoin the party. I may or may not have smelled the soap and shampoo in the shower to see if I could discover what gave Brett his irresistible smell. I found a bottle of cologne and tried to pick out the individual scents: blackberry, pear, ginger, rosemary and sandalwood. Then someone started banging on the bathroom door.

"Just a minute," I yelled. I gave my reflection a last glance before leaving the bathroom. When I pulled the door open I almost ran into Courtney Elsweed, captain of the senior volleyball team, and just about the most popular girl in our school. Not to mention Brett's new girlfriend, though I hadn't verified the rumors with my own eyes. She scowled at me.

"I've been waiting for five minutes. What are you even doing here, anyway? This is a *senior* party," she said, storming past me and slamming the door.

Out in the dark hall, alone, I decided to find Crys and tell her I was going home. I crept around upstairs until I heard voices coming from one room. Lots of voices, laughing, so it probably wasn't an orgy. I pushed the door open. The room was dark and filled with smoke. I almost stumbled on the circle of bodies sitting on the ground. Brett and some of his friends sat on the floor, passing a bong. Crys was sitting next to Cody, with a big grin on her face.

"You can come in if you want, but can you decide quickly, and shut the door?" Brett said.

* * *

I was tempted to run away and hide somewhere, but anger at Crys drove me forward. I squeezed into the circle next to her.

"Nice of you to tell me where you were," I whispered, crossing my arms and frowning at her.

"I didn't think you'd be into this," she shrugged.

She had a point. In Middle School I was president of the Drug Awareness group; we worked with the local police to warn kids away from using drugs. In high school however, my stance had mellowed. I knew Crys smoked pot sometimes, and most of the other kids I knew had tried harder stuff. They didn't go crazy, or jump out of windows, or steal and lie to their families. I realized that most of the stories I'd been told had been inflated.

That didn't mean I was eager to try it myself. I still considered smoking and drinking to be pretty stupid; in my opinion they made you idiotic, accident prone and potentially dead, if you used them long enough.

The bong had made it around the circle and was passed to me. To my side, Crys reached for it, but I took it into my hands.

"You don't have to smoke if you don't want to," Brett said.

If anything was going to happen with Brett, it would be tonight. Getting his attention might warrant a bold move. I held out my hand for the lighter and tried to remember what I'd seen everyone else do.

I held the flame up to the small bowl of purplish green dried leaves, and watched them begin to glow and burn, tossing out rolls of thick white smoke. Then I sucked in the smoke and tried to hold it in as long as I could—which was only a couple of seconds before I started coughing violently. The others laughed, but before I could feel embarrassed, Brett smiled at me.

"That's totally normal, it happens to everyone the first time," he said.

"It's good, actually," Cody said, "coughing will get you higher."

I passed the bong to Crys and smiled coyly at Brett, who was nodding his approval. Crys gave me a half hug before preparing the bong for another hit.

My lungs burned, and I felt like I had tar on the inside of my throat. But after a few minutes, my anxiety dissolved. Then I started to feel *really* good.

I don't know if it was the weed, or just that I was sitting in a room with my best friend and the coolest seniors at my school, doing something against the rules. In *Brett Peter's* room, no less. I looked around, soaking it in. He had a bookshelf, with some of the books from English class and then a few others that surprised me. *Romantic poets?* I looked over and caught his eye, and flashed him a wide smile. He gave me a knowing look and smiled back.

That's when the room went pink.

It started out low, like waves of pink and orange flame moving up the walls from the ground. Then it crept in, closer, wrapping around the furniture, and slowly crawling over the arms and legs of my classmates. By the time it started to wrap around their heads like a thick pink fog, blurring and distorting their features, my smile was gone and my eyes were open wide.

This isn't just pot.

Pot wasn't supposed to be hallucinogenic. Maybe they mixed it with something else. Maybe this was a practical joke of some kind. *Be cool.* Crys wouldn't let anything bad happen to me. I took a deep breath and steeled myself for an adventure.

No matter what happens, none of this is real.

The bodies and limbs and faces around me disappeared. Then the furniture started moving around. A hole appeared in the ceiling, through which I could see stars. A dark stain spread down the wall. The furniture rusted, fell over and broke apart. Then a thick layer of dust covered everything in the room, turning it ash gray. When the flames stopped dancing and my vision returned to normal, I was still in Brett's room. I could see the walls in the dim light, and even one of the posters he had hanging, though it was ripped now. Someone had smashed up the desk to remove the drawers. And I was completely alone:

so alone that I could hear my heart pounding and feel the hairs on my arms stand on end.

I pinched myself, hard, and felt the pain radiating up my arm. Goosebumps covered my body.

I cupped my hands over my ears, testing them out. They seemed to be functioning normally, but I couldn't hear Cody joking around or Crys laughing. There was a slight whistling noise from the breeze passing through the layers of ripped installation from the open section of the ceiling. But the thing that scared me the worst was the smell of earthy moss and cat urine. I don't remember ever smelling things in my dreams.

This isn't real.

I reached out beside me and tried to find Crys, but my hand came down on bits of broken glass and a layer of dead leaves and dirt. I stood up cautiously, expecting my body to be off balance. I didn't want to make a fool of myself by acting weird. The other kids could probably see me, even if I couldn't see them. But my depth perception and movement seemed fine. I put my arms out to my sides, then brought my index finger in and touched my nose. As far as I could tell, I was totally normal.

Nobody cried out as I made my way across the room. Two of the shelves were broken and had dumped their contents on the floor. The third held a handful of items. A plastic baseball trophy from 2009. The top of it—a golden figurine of a player swinging a bat—had broken off and fallen. I picked it up from the floor. There was a model of a sports car with one door missing. The paint was chipped and what may have once been red was a patchy orange color. There was also a thick book.

I picked it up and blew off the layer of dust. *A yearbook.* I flipped through it and recognized some faces. Then I checked the cover.

ELLISVILLE HIGH SCHOOL, 2015-2016

That's this school year. This yearbook shouldn't be out for months.

I wondered if Brett got an early copy somehow. I opened the book again and looked through more closely. When I got to the full page photo spread in the middle, I froze. It was me, wearing a formal dress and laughing. Next to me was Brett in a Tux, with his arm around me. The caption said, *Prom Queen and King.*

That would have been more surprising if I hadn't already had dreams of this kind before. But never as vivid as this one. I could feel the canvas texture of the book in my hand. A chilly breeze made me shiver in the darkness. My sweater was still around my waist so I shrugged it on.

I heard the hoot of an owl outside. It was creepy, but not terrifying. I've had lucid dreams before, as well as a few bouts of night terrors when I was younger, but this was new territory. I tried to rationalize it. Obviously this is some kind of wish fulfillment, my subconscious creating a fiction based on my desires. It was triggered by smoking. But I'm probably fine, and safe. *Just keep calm.*

On an impulse, I tore the picture of Brett and me out of the book and stuffed it in my pocket. Then I flipped to the back and looked through the photos of my classmates. Most of them looked like I expected them to. One girl, Brandi Thompson, was wearing braces, though I don't think she really has them. Another, Jennifer

Crawford, had a ridiculous bowl cut. I'd always seen her with long brown hair.

Weird.

I put the book down and opened the door to the room. The hallway was dark and the air so musty I could hardly breathe. It was almost pitch black, except for the faint starlight coming in through the ceiling behind me. The railing down the stairs was broken. The carpet looked like hell. It had been cream originally, but was now patchy and stained. There was a large, dark red stain in the center of the hall that made my skin crawl.

The floorboards creaked under my sneakers, even though I was basically tip-toeing around. I noticed again how *quiet* it was. Westwood was a reasonably peaceful suburb, but it was never totally silent; the hum of modern life, cars driving by, someone with a TV or radio on—there was always something. But not here. I crossed the hall into another bedroom, looking for a window that faced East. I found one and pulled the blinds to the side.

We were only about ten miles outside of St. Louis. I should be able to see the glow of the city lights on the horizon, but there was nothing. Just darkness, as far as the eye could see, apart from the stars, which shone more brightly than I'd ever seen them. This must be Brett's parents' bedroom. There were shards of glass sprinkled throughout the dark carpet, from a standing mirror that had fallen over and smashed. They twinkled like tiny stars, reflecting the night sky.

I stepped on something hard and bent over to pick it up. It was a small family photo, in a homemade frame that had been decorated with macaroni. On the back was some childish handwriting. *To Mom, love Brett. Age 5.*

There was a bit more light downstairs, due to the windows on all sides of the house and the full moon. One of the windows had been smashed in and vines and shrubs were reaching into the living room like an invading alien species. In the kitchen, most of the cabinet doors were open, the shelves empty. I stumbled against the fridge, which was unplugged and on its side. I tried flicking the light switch on the kitchen wall but nothing happened.

Then I heard the sound of the floorboards creaking under someone's weight. Not *my* weight. My heart pounded in my chest and my throat tightened.

"*Hello?*" I called softly.

It suddenly occurred to me that this was exactly the type of house where you'd find ghosts or an axe-murderer. I was breathing as quietly as I could, and the lack of oxygen didn't do anything to calm me down. I felt sweat on my skin, which tingled in the cold air. I thought about all the fairy tales I knew of, seeking a way to wake myself up. I tried clicking my heels together three times. I imagined an "eat me" cake to restore normalcy but none appeared.

My eyes were adjusting to the darkness, and I thought I could make out a pale shape in the corner. A shape that kind of looked like a naked man. And in the darkness, I thought I could see his shoulders rising up and down with every breath, and large, inhuman eyes that seemed to glow in the darkness.

There was a flash of movement as the shape threw itself at me out of the darkness. I caught a glimpse of pale skin and large grey eyes, just before I shrieked and turned to run. I'd only gone a step when I heard a sharp *thwap*. I cried out as the shape sailed past me, crashing into the cupboards with a hideous screeching, like a metal desk being dragged across a stone floor. The creature left spurts of blood on the countertop, then fell into a pile on the floor, one thin wrist twitching before it was completely still. The creature's blood was black like tar and smelled like copper.

My hands were shaking as I yanked open the kitchen drawers, searching franticly for a weapon. I pulled out the best thing I could find—a heavy wooden rolling pin. I brandished it in front of me just as another dark shadow moved towards me.

"And just what do you think you're going to do with that?" a voice asked. "Bakeoff?"

2

He was wearing all black and gray, but faded, like denim after it's been washed too much. Jean and leather mostly, but I could tell it had been ripped and patched up again. Imperfectly, like he'd done the repairs himself and didn't give a shit about how he looked. His cargo pants were baggy around the crotch but then tightened at the ankles, stuffed into a pair of black combat boots. There were far more pockets and extra straps than seemed necessary. His belt held a hunting knife on one side and a holster in the other. The gleam of metal told me he was carrying a pistol.

His hood kept his face in shadow, but I could tell he was young—less than twenty for sure. I could see the tips of his long dark hair poking out from beneath his chin. His hands and most of his arms were covered by what I suspected was a pair of socks with holes cut into them for his fingers, and he clutched a crossbow loosely at his side.

He brushed past me, ignoring my defensive stance and the rolling pin, and grabbed the arrow jutting out from the creature behind me. He twisted it out with a sharp pull, and flicked the black blood off before sticking the arrow back in his quiver. I shuddered. Then he headed to the front door, which I could see was open.

“We’ve got to move,” he said, gesturing behind him for me to follow.

I didn’t budge. I was staring at the grotesque body behind me.

“What is this thing?” I asked. It was humanoid, but with leathery skin, almost no hair, and fingers like talons. Curved and edged with sharp, hard nails.

“You’ve never seen a modified before?” The boy eyed me with surprise, then confusion. “Have you been living in a cave your whole life?”

"Who are you?" I asked.

"The guy who just saved your life," he said. "Now shut up and stick behind me." He walked to the front door, raising his crossbow in front of him. The long grass and weeds in the front lawn came up to his knees, and shimmered like a wheat field in the moonlight as he crossed through them.

I hesitated on the front porch. At least the house was familiar. I followed him to the edge of the yard but stopped at the street. What if I was sleep walking or something? I didn't want to get run over. That's when I saw the cars. Several were parked awkwardly or just sitting in the middle of the street. One had swerved into the curb just in front of Brett's house and crashed into a mailbox, which was bent downwards. The window was smashed in, and the driver's body had been pulled halfway through the window. But all that was left of the driver was a skeleton, and some scraps of the clothes he'd been wearing. His left arm had been ripped off—the bones were lying a few feet away from the car.

There was another figure in the passenger seat. From the strands of long hair still stuck to her gleaming white skull, and the remains of a purple dress, it was all that was left of a little girl. Her jawbone was unhinged and hanging at an awkward angle, and her bony arms were still clutching a doll tightly. I felt vomit rise up in my throat. I stumbled back and fell on my hands and knees, heaving.

The boy came up beside me. Past the smell of my own vomit, I could smell his scent. Musk, pine trees, and smoke, like from a campfire.

"Are you sick? I've got some meds back at my camp—"

I looked back at him, my brows knitted together.

"There's a dead guy, *right there*. And a little girl," my words caught in my throat and my eyes burned.

"Can't you see them?"

"Yeah but that happened ages ago," he shrugged. "During the Modification. Those bodies will have been picked clean by now, nothing useful on them."

The world was spinning and I felt weak.

"Don't tell me you haven't seen a remnant before," he said. "They're all over. In the city there are piles of them. Some people use them to make fences."

My lip curled in disgust. I couldn't tell if he was kidding. If he was it was in poor taste. Those were *people.* I was getting so worked up I almost believed this was all really happening. *It's just a dream,* I told myself, sitting on the grass, my arms wrapped around me. He frowned at me, casting looks in both direction.

"Mods hunt in small groups, usually four or five at a time. That one wasn't alone, and the others will probably be here any second. So if you don't want to die, come with me. But if you do want to die, or you've gone crazy, I'm not going to risk my neck for you. You've got five seconds to make a choice."

He reached his hand down, towards me.

I didn't know what was going on, but something about the boy made me feel safe. And he had just saved me, right? I reached up tentatively. He grabbed my arm and hoisted me up.

"Now, unless you're attached to that rolling pin..." he said, pulling out his hunting knife, "this might be more practical." He flipped it in the air and caught it by the blade, holding the handle out towards me. My arm dipped as I took it from him. It was heavier than I expected. It felt so... *solid.* I ran a finger over the edge and cried out as I felt the blade bite into my skin. Blood welled up in the cut. I put my finger in my mouth. The blood was tangy and metallic against my tongue.

"This is... *real.*" I said.

"Um, yeah," he said, frowning.

Out of the corner of my eye I saw several more dark shapes materialize out of the trees, and heard another blood-curdling screech. But I also saw the pink flickers again, and smiled.

Finally.

I woke up gasping for breath, my eyes rolling. Everything was white. I thought maybe I'd gone blind, but after blinking a few times my vision cleared.

I was back in Brett's room, but the lights were on. I'd never been happier to see a functioning lightbulb. Crys was crying and squeezing me with her arms. Brett's face was white, but he looked relieved.

"What happened?" I asked weakly, pulling my hair out of my face.

"You passed out," Crys said.

"I was just about to get my dad to drive you to the ER, or call 911," Brett said.

"I told you all, she was fine," Cody said, like he'd made this argument a dozen times.

"We checked your pulse," Crys said. "We thought you were—that you might be... Do you feel okay?"

I sat up and looked around, suddenly aware of everybody's eyes on me.

"Yeah, I'm fine. Sorry..."

"It's not your fault," Brett said, "Though we were really worried about you. I mean if anything happened..."

"We would have been busted," Cody interrupted, nodding his head. "Like, for real. We aren't even supposed to have this shit."

"And we didn't know if, maybe we were just being paranoid, you know. We're not in the right frame of mind to be making emergency decisions. So I was going to get my dad, even though he would have killed me, but then... then you woke up," Brett said, running his hands through his hair in the way that I'd always found irresistible. I realized now he did it when he was nervous.

I stood up. Crys grabbed my arm but I wasn't dizzy or shaky. I saw the red model car on the shelf. *Had I noticed that when I came in?* I must have. I didn't see any yearbook though.

"We even looked it up," Crys said, showing me the laptop on the desk. "We Googled *passing out on weed* and it's not unheard of... this guy says it's called 'pulling a whitey', which means you smoked too much too quickly and it made your blood pressure drop. But it isn't fatal, you're supposed to just stay calm and just ride it out."

I nodded, unsure if I should feel glad they looked it up or angry that they hadn't just gone for help. But then I was relieved they didn't. How much more of a loser would I be if I'd gotten everybody in trouble for smoking?

"Did you see white?" Brett asked. "That's what happens if your blood pressure drops too fast."

"I'm...I'm not sure." I saw pink. But I didn't say anything. "How long was I out for?"

"Just five minutes or so, but it was really scary. I couldn't get you to wake up. I even tried slapping you," Crys said.

I put one hand up to my cheek. She'd slapped me and I hadn't felt anything?

"Well, anyway, I'm fine now. Just a little... weak."

"You guys should go home," Brett said. I looked at Crys and she nodded.

There were more people than I remembered downstairs. The party was just getting started, and I was already leaving. Courtney was in the living room with her friends. When I passed near them on my way to the door, I heard her fake-cough, "*slut*." When I looked up, everybody was looking at me, and her friends were laughing. My cheeks burned.

Crys strode up to Courtney and shoved her backwards. She grabbed two of her friends and held onto their arms as she tipped over the coffee table and landed hard on the ground, with half a dozen plastic cups and bottles raining down on top of her.

“Run,” Crys whispered, grabbing my arm and shoving me out the door. We raced to the car and jumped in, breathless. Crys turned the key and revved the engine, then we peeled around the corner and took off. After we’d gone a couple blocks, we looked at each other and laughed.

“That’s totally going to cost me,” Crys said.

“What do you think’s going to happen?” I asked.

“I can’t see us duking it out in the parking lot,” Crys said. “She wouldn’t want to break a nail.”

“I’d rather take a punch than be on her wrong side,” I said. “Courtney could make your life miserable.”

“It was worth it to see the expression on her face when she fell over the table,” Crys said, grinning. “And anyway, she’s graduating at the end of the year. I don’t care what she does.”

Crys pulled up my driveway and let me out.

“Sorry I ruined the party,” I said.

"Are you kidding, I had a blast," she smiled. "Glad you're okay."

Apart from hating myself for blowing my one shot with Brett, I felt fine. I'd pretty much convinced myself that smoking had given me a crazy vivid dream.

Except for one thing.

As the van pulled away, I held up my finger, which had been throbbing since my adventure. In the street lights I could see a very clean, but very real, cut on the tip of my finger.

3

I woke up with a groan as scenes from last night jumbled together in my brain. I must have just cut my finger on something while I was passed out in Brett's room. Then in the dream I imagined cutting myself with the knife. That's how dreams worked, right? Anyway I had more important things to worry about. Like how I'd gone from being invisible to notorious in one evening. If I was going to try pot, it should have been in a private, safe environment, with just Crys or trusted friends. Not Brett Peters and a bunch of other seniors. They're all going to think I'm a total loser. I basically crashed a party I wasn't even invited to, let myself into a smoking session I'd deliberately been excluded from, and then spazzed out, embarrassing myself in front of everybody I'd been wanting to impress.

Which, collectively, didn't totally suck. I mean, until yesterday they didn't know me at all. Now they knew me and didn't like me. It wouldn't actually change my life very much. It's not like we'd been hanging out anyway. But then the thing with Courtney... had she really called me a slut? What for—I hadn't done anything. For a second I panicked, thinking something might have happened while I was passed out. I remember a story about a girl who got drunk, and then guys shared pictures of them taking advantage of her while she was unconscious. *There could be naked pictures of me out there right now.* But Crys had been there the whole time, there's no way she'd have let that happen. I don't know how I got on Courtney's radar, but after what Crys did to her, in front of everybody, Monday was bound to be unpleasant.

I comforted myself with waffles. I put a frozen Eggo in the toaster, then covered it in butter, syrup and whipped cream when it was done. Then added blueberries and raspberries. I washed it down with a mug of hot chocolate, until my anxiety faded to a dull ache. I had homework to do, but there was no way I'd be able to focus on math or grammar. Instead I started sorting out the recycling, tossing cans, bottles, paper and glass into the right receptacles. Dad did it sometimes, but he always left it until really late Sunday night. A procrastinator, like me.

I wheeled the recycling bin down the driveway. It was chilly outside. I could see my breath. I crossed my arms as I headed back to the house. I glanced sideways and saw my neighbor Eric raking leaves next door. He was wearing headphones and pretending he didn't see me. Eric was a year older than me and had curly, auburn hair and freckles. As neighbors the same age, our parents had made us play together when we were little, and we were pretty good friends when we were ten. We'd geek out about comic books and pretend we had super powers. But we've been weird since middle school. We had different circles of friends and had even stopped saying "hi" when we passed each other in the halls.

Back inside the house, I did the dishes and straightened my room. Then my hands ran out of things to do, and I couldn't keep the images of last night out of my head any longer. The dilapidated house. The little girl in the car. The dark gaping holes of her eye sockets, her jaw hanging open in a silent scream. And that monster that had attacked me. His huge, grotesque eyes. His unnaturally long, skinny fingers. I shuddered. I lay on my bed listening to music and looking up *smoking + hallucinations* on my phone. I couldn't call it a hallucination, I found out, since I was unconscious. But I *was* conscious, kind of, just not here in the real world.

Dream didn't feel like the right word either. From what I could tell, it seemed more like an acid trip. People often report very brief experiences that can seem like they last forever, a time distortion effect.

My trip was like that—Crys said I'd only been out for a few minutes, but it had felt like at least an hour. Plus it had felt so real. I reached again for my jeans pocket, turning it inside out like I'd already done several times, but I couldn't find the picture I'd torn from the yearbook. *Obviously*, because of course it hadn't actually happened. Me and Brett, Prom King and Queen? *Yeah right.* It was already November, so we'd have to start dating pretty soon. That's not likely—considering he'll probably never talk to me again.

But I couldn't let it go. I put on a coat and a scarf and went back outside. Eric looked up as I approached, and took off his headphones.

"Keeping warm?" I said.

"Yeah, sure," he said, blowing on his hands. But he didn't smile. His expression said *what do you want?*

"I know we haven't talked for a long time, but I've been dealing with something and I thought you might be able to help me," I said.

He raised his eyebrows. "Shoot," he said. But he looked worried, like I was going to ask him a big favor.

"What do you know about time travel?" I asked.

"For real?" he said, looking around. "This isn't a prank? No hidden cameras?"

"I wouldn't do that to you," I said quietly.

He looked me over, but finally seemed satisfied.

"Well in that case," he said, lifting the corners of his mouth, "I think we need some tea."

I hadn't been in Eric's room for five years. Most of the toys and action figures were gone, replaced by books and a sprawling computer system with two monitors. He pulled a book off the shelf and tossed it at me.

"Start with that," he said. "*The Time Machine* by H. G. Wells. A classic. Can't go wrong. Can I ask why you're interested?"

"I had this crazy dream..." I said. "It was just so *real*. I can't get it out of my head."

I followed him downstairs, where he put on an electric kettle.

"So in this dream," he said, reaching for a pair of mugs, "you thought you were in the future? How could you tell?"

I took a deep breath in relief. I didn't realize how badly I'd needed to talk about this. Crys would have just told me to forget about it.

"I was in the future, but it was all ruined, like... abandoned. And there were dead people; skeletons. And monsters..."

"Sounds like your typical post-apocalyptic novel," he grinned. "Maybe you've been reading too much—or waiting for the movies to come out, if that's your thing now."

There was a sharpness in his voice: a disapproval that said *I don't know who you are anymore*. But I ignored it.

"Yeah but the details," I continued. "I flipped through a book and I could read it. I picked up something from the ground. I felt chilly, I smelled things, I had conversations—"

I cut myself with a knife. I pressed my lips together.

"Anything different about your diet or habits?" he asked. "Something that would affect your sleep?" Of course Eric was going to jump straight to the most rational answer. But maybe that's why I was here.

"You don't think it's possible to see the future, to have visions?"

"I don't believe in dreams and prophecies, if that's what you're asking. That stuff usually is just wish-fulfillment and seeing patterns where none exist. Usually fortune tellers just feed you vague bullshit that will probably happen, or at least make you feel good in the present. Or else something you'll have to interpret later, so when something happens to you, you'll think back and say *aha, so that's what she was talking about.*"

"So, skeptic, then."

"Yeah, about that kind of stuff. But real time travel? Scientifically? Doesn't seem impossible. Maybe time is a dimension that we don't understand yet. We still barely understand space, or normal physics. Time is relative. If you take a long space voyage and come back to earth, more time will have passed on earth than you've experienced. So one year for you could be one hundred years for the people on earth."

"I didn't dream about spaceships... I was still on earth." In Brett Peter's house.

"But time travel machines might work a similar way. Or maybe you don't even need a machine. Did you ever read *Stitches in Time*?"

"Um, no," I said, holding my tea cup with both hands and enjoying the warmth on my fingers. "Missed that one."

"Classic book... it's about how, maybe time and space can be folded up, like a piece of paper, and you can pass through from one point to the other. Maybe you just have to know how to do it, and concentrate."

"If you did see the future, is there any way to prove whether or not it was real?" I asked.

"Sure," Eric nodded. "Did you see anything different about the future that doesn't match with reality? If so, you just need to wait for that thing to happen. Though it isn't likely anybody will believe you after the fact. To be safe, you should write those things down in a sealed envelope, and ask someone else to keep it for you. Otherwise, you can't be sure that you aren't just fooling yourself."

"Um... but also... I was kind of with some other people, and they stayed with me. So... it means my body was still here in the present, when I was in the future."

"Wait, you were sleeping with other people?" he asked.

"I was at a party, and I kind of passed out."

"You *passed out*?" his eyes widened. "How much were you drinking?"

"Not a lot, okay? And I'm fine. I had like, one drink and one hit of the bong."

"Weed?" Eric frowned. He looked like he was disappointed in me.

The leaf had actually looked more like a purple flower. Did anybody at the party actually *say* it was weed, or had I just assumed that?

"Maybe," I said.

"So this wasn't a dream."

"I don't know what it was, okay? I'm just—I don't have anybody else to talk to about this, and you're good with weird."

We glared at each other for a second, but then he laughed.

"Thanks, I think." He pushed his glasses up the bridge of his nose.

"Fine," he said, leaning his elbows on the table. "Let's figure this out. Could you interact with objects?"

"Yes, I picked up a book and looked through it. And I held... other objects."

"So you were corporeal. What were you wearing?"

"Huh?"

"Did you have clothes on? Were they the same clothes you had on when you had the dream? Maybe it was a duplicate of you, in a different timeline. You travelled, but the you of this timeline was still here. Just an additional version of you entered into a future timeline."

"You mean, I took over future me's body? I don't think so. I was wearing the same clothes. I put something in my pocket too, but it wasn't there when I woke up." I thought that was the smoking gun, that proved I'd made it all up, but it didn't faze Eric.

"That doesn't mean anything. Maybe the thing in the future didn't exist yet in the past. Maybe you can't bring anything backwards with you into the present. Next time you party too hard, see if you can bring anything with you into the future."

"There won't be a next time," I said. "Does this mean you believe me?"

"Not even a little bit," he smiled. He was making fun of me.

I pushed off from the counter stool and put the mug back on the counter. "Thanks for the tea. I've got some homework to do."

"Yeah, um, sure," Eric held the front door open for me. "Listen, Alicia, if you have any more weird dreams... it was nice to talk with you again." He looked sad. For a second I thought he was going to say something mushy like *I've missed hanging out with you.* I threw my scarf over my shoulder and left before he could.

* * *

My older sister, Tamara, showed up that night with Chinese food. She usually brought dinner on Sunday nights, it was our weekly family time. She was a Junior at a liberal arts school in St. Louis. We used to have fun together, but she changed after mom died. I'd been really young, and Tamara had basically raised me on her own while Dad worked. After graduation, she could have gone anywhere in the country, but she stayed nearby, I think to keep tabs on Dad and I and make sure everything was going okay.

Now she used all her energy to save the world. She was always talking about some protest she was organizing, usually about the environment. I pushed the food around on my plate as she launched into another one of her rants.

"It's insane, they take all these soybeans and they genetically modify them to be stronger and more resistant to bugs and stuff. But then they put pressure on all the farmers to use their strain of soybeans. And if they don't, they get thugs to go in and vandalize the property."

"That's hard to believe," my dad said, rubbing his chin. "Sounds like rumormongering to me. I don't suppose anything like that has been proven."

"If not then why would anybody else be bothering poor farmers? Who picks on farmers? It's because they are trying to hold out, they just want to work hard and make a decent living, good people, you know—but these huge corporations come in and say, you have to use our strain of vegetables, and buy directly from us, and pay us a percentage of your earnings. And the ones that say no, they start having accidents, until they go out of business. You think that's coincidence? Bad luck? No way. Zamonta knows exactly what they're doing. They're putting everybody else out of business. And that means soon, there won't be any locally produced, non-GMO produce available. No organic apples or pears. Just the Franken-Fruit. Identical. Pest-resistant."

I rolled my eyes. I'd heard kids talk about stuff like this at school, but I'd never bought into it.

"What's so bad about pest-resistant fruit?" I asked. "Doesn't that mean they can use less pesticides? Isn't that good?" I didn't really care one way or another, but something about my sister's certainty always made me want to poke holes in her arguments. That much certainty could be dangerous. She dodged my question with another fact, something she always did that pissed me off.

"Did you know that we throw away almost 40% of our food, before we even eat it? We have such a warped idea about what a peach is these days, if it's not just perfect, farmers let it rot on the ground."

"What's that got to do with anything?" I asked.

"We're wasting perfectly good food," Tamara snapped, "because of some ideal shape we've decided peaches have to be, even though the other ones are just as good."

I opened my mouth to tell her that argument didn't make any sense, but Dad interrupted.

"I'm sure it's complicated," he said, holding up his hands to calm down the fight he could smell brewing.

"Anyway," Tamara continued, glaring at me, "we're organizing a debate with one of the representatives. I think normally they'd turn down this kind of thing but because he's local and I'm local, they think it'd be a good idea. They really need local support. They've got enough money to buy out anybody else, but if the community in this area is against them... I mean they've got their main headquarters here, this is where they do most of their research and testing. Did you even know that? This is about the debate." She pulled some fliers out of her bag and slid them across the table.

"It'll be a city council meeting, open to everybody. See if you can get some friends at your high school to come, or just pass these out." She nodded at the stack of fliers and I picked one up.

"Um, sure," I said. My friends wouldn't go, and I probably wouldn't go either, but I could pretend if it meant getting through dinner. The flier read like a conspiracy theorist's wet dream.

> *Is Zamonta destroying the world? Are genetically modified foods really safe? Find out! We will ask the tough questions, and put the world's biggest source of consumable genetic modification on trial for the first time ever, in this public debate.*

My eyes latched onto the word *modification* and I reread the sentence slowly. But it seemed harmless. My sister's name was listed as well as the Zamonta representative she'd be debating. My fork froze halfway to my mouth, danging chow mein.

"Kyle Peters?" I asked.

"You know him?" Tamara said.

"I think... I go to school with his son," I said. I didn't mention I had psychotic breakdown at his house last night.

"Could be, he probably lives around here, the company isn't far away. You should come. I think most people don't even know what goes on back there, what they're really researching or working on. We need to put some pressure on them, so they know people care about what they eat."

I nodded. *Maybe Brett would be there.* Suddenly I wondered where Brett had gotten the weed from, if it had really been weed at all.

4

I was walking my bike out of the garage Monday morning when I saw Brett's black jeep parked outside my house. My heart pounded as I wheeled over to him. *What was he doing here?*

He rolled down the window and grinned at me, like showing up at my house at 7:30am was totally normal.

"Um, hi," I said.

"Thought you might need a ride," he said. He looked perfect, as always, with khakis and a dark blue button-down.

"I've got a bike," I said lamely. *He can see that, idiot.*

"Yeah but after what happened Saturday, maybe you should take it easy for a few days. Right?"

I shrugged. Brett Peters wanted to give me a lift to school. Why was I being difficult?

"Let me just put my bike away," I said quickly. I threw my bike in the garage and locked the door behind me. My palms were sweaty as I opened up the passenger door and climbed in next to Brett. I thought Courtney and her friends were going to pop out from somewhere and prank me, but the back seat was empty.

I held my hands up to the heater, blowing warm air on my fingers. Even the seats were heated. I don't think I'd ever been in a car this nice. I calmed down after we'd driven a few blocks, but my mind was still racing. *Was this really happening?*

"So, I just wanted to make sure you were okay," Brett said. "And let you know, you know, I'm really sorry. And if you need anything, or have any problems, you can come talk to me about them."

I nodded, unsure what he wanted from me.

"I just don't want this to turn into a big deal, or become a problem later on..." he said.

Oh. So that's why he picked me up. He was afraid I'd tell someone, or that our family would sue his family or something. He was doing damage control. My chest ached with disappointment, and then I felt stupid for letting it get to me. What had I expected? This wasn't a fairy tale. Guys like Brett didn't date girls like me.

"Also, it would be really bad if my dad found out about this. Really, *really* bad. I kind of stole that stuff from him."

"It wasn't marijuana?" I asked.

"I thought it was," Brett said. "But after what happened to you, I did some research. Now I'm not so sure. But, basically this has to disappear. I don't want the whole school talking about how we smoked at my house. My dad could get in a lot of trouble. So could I."

"I'm not going to tell anyone," I said, sinking lower into the chair and looking out the window. *He thinks I'm a gossip and a snitch.*

"I'd get in trouble too. And it wasn't exactly my most glorious moment. It's not something I'd go bragging about."

He smiled. It hit me like a warm ray of sun, even though it was gray and dreary outside.

"Great," he said. "The less anybody knows about what happened, the better. For both of us."

He pulled into the parking lot and we got out of the jeep. Courtney and her friends were waiting near the main doors. She saw us coming, and her eyes widened. Part of me felt smug. I knew she was going to freak out about Brett giving me a ride. Another part of me panicked. Even if Courtney had been willing to forget about what happened at the party, she wasn't going to let this slide.

"Thanks for the ride," I said, "see you later." I darted away from Brett, feeling Courtney's eyes burning a hole in my back as I headed around the building to one of the side entrances. No point in provoking Courtney before Brett had a chance to smooth things over.

The picture I'd seen in my vision popped into my mind again. *Prom king and queen*. Even though I was still sure it could never happen, it didn't seem as totally impossible as it had yesterday. I mean, at least he knew my name now.

Even if he did think I was a tattle-tale. But then I remembered the skeleton. The dead girl with the doll. If there was even a miniscule chance that what I'd seen in the yearbook was real, did that mean everything else could be as well?

I decided to take Eric's advice, even though it seemed crazy. I wrote down a few of the things I'd seen in my vision; things that would be easy to verify. Then I folded up the paper into a crude envelope and sealed it with tape. I handed it to Crys during first period.

"What's this? Party invitation?" she said.

"It's... an experiment. Don't open it. Just keep it, hide it somewhere. Make sure there's no way I could find it or change anything. Actually—sign your name over the fold on the back so you'll know if it's been opened."

"Like a magic trick?" she raised one eyebrow at me. "Aren't you a little old for this kind of stuff?"

"Just do it. Please?" I said.

She shrugged, then pulled out a pen and signed her name. She put the sealed paper in her backpack. When she was done, she smiled at me and gave me a knowing look.

"I heard a rumor that Brett gave you a ride to school. Please tell me it's true." I couldn't control my mouth as it smiled back at her. She raised her palm to high-five me. The butterflies did celebratory flips and dances in my stomach.

"It's not what you think," I said. "He just wanted to make sure I wouldn't tell anyone what happened. He's afraid of getting in trouble."

"The ship might have sailed on that one," Crys said. "It's all over school already."

My face paled and I grabbed her wrist. "What, exactly?"

"A rumor. About you. Want to hear it? I wasn't sure if I should tell you, but it's probably better to know, instead of having people talk behind your back. Right?"

I gulped, then nodded. This was going to be bad.

"Courtney is *pissed.* She hated me already, cuz I'm with Cody, but she just thinks Cody is using me, and that it's not serious. She thinks he'll tire of me. So she's been tolerating me, because she has her sights on Brett anyway. But then, I was upstairs with the boys at the party, and then you came in too. So now all her friends are saying you and I were letting the boys double team us or something, you know, sophomore skanks."

The blood drained from my face, and it was suddenly hard to breathe. People thought I was a skank? I'd barely gotten to second base.

"But that's not the rumor," she continued. "One of the boys in the room is dating one of Courtney's friends, so when he came back down, she was yelling at him, throwing a fit, asking why he'd been gone so long. And he told her that we were all smoking, but that you'd passed out, and everybody was freaking out and trying to revive you until you came to again. I think he needed to lay it on thick to convince her he hadn't cheated on her with one of us. So then I heard this other rumor today about how you faked being passed out at Brett's party to get him to notice you."

Wait—what? My eyes went wide in surprise. "People think I'm a slut, and also that I faked passing out for attention?"

"I know, right? It doesn't even make sense. The two rumors can't both be true. Nobody who was in that room would have started a rumor like that, that's so totally not what really happened. But if

Courtney likes Brett, then she wouldn't have been eager to feel sorry for you, and might have said something mean, like, 'I bet she faked it for attention,' and someone might have overheard that..."

I nodded. "You've really got this high school rumor mill thing down to a science."

"I know," she said, smiling. "I'm awesome. People have been talking shit about me for years. It used to stress me out, but it helps to know who started the rumors, and why. Courtney is just feeling threatened because a cute sophomore caught Brett's attention. And either she's totally crazy, or Brett actually likes you a little bit. Either way, it's not a big deal. Well, at least it's not negative."

Not negative? I was mortified. Crys might be able to shrug it off, but how could I walk around school like everything was normal, knowing people were saying these awful things about me? And why would passing out make Brett like me more? It didn't make any sense. If anything, he felt sorry for me. Or was annoyed. He probably wished Crys hadn't brought me with her. Or maybe he was afraid I'd tell my parents and he'd get in major trouble for offering me drugs.

Or maybe he *did* like me. I fixated on this until lunch, because it made me feel a little better. I may or may not have even started sketching his face from memory and writing his name in my notebook repeatedly, something I hadn't done for a while.

I kept my head down in class, with my hood up and earphones on. *Ignore everybody for a few weeks, and it will all blow over.* I just had to stay out of Courtney's way, and avoid doing anything that drew more attention to myself.

After lunch I had gym class. I'd like to make the argument that varsity athletes made; that gym was a waste of time because they got plenty of exercise in their extracurricular activities. But I didn't play any sports. The truth is, I hated gym because I hated running. Or moving my body quickly, at all. I had the reflexes of a doorstop, which made me inevitably horrible at any and all sports. I could do most of the challenges: rope climb, pushups, crunchies… but toss me into a team sport and my team would lose. I changed into my gym clothes, shorts and a t-shirt, and followed the other girls out onto the court.

We were playing volleyball. Not my least favorite, by a long shot. In basketball and soccer, you had to run around constantly, even if you didn't have the ball. The teacher yelled at you to "pick up the pace" and "look alive."

In volleyball you just stood there. I was pretty great at that part. But then there was the other part—what happened when the ball came right at you, and it was obviously yours. You were supposed to yell "I go" and then spike it, set it or bump it. We'd learned the terms at the beginning of the semester. I did okay if I was just practicing with a partner; usually Crys and I could get the ball back and forth between us five or six times, bumping it with our forearms.

But in a game, I panicked. Everything moved too quickly, and I'd hit the ball wrong, and it would shoot off to the side or hit another team member in the head. The other girls in my class had learned to duck, or better yet to steal the ball from me.

But today, when the whistle blew to start the game, something was... different. The opposing team served the ball. It came over to our side and one girl hit it back over the net, then someone on the other side gave it a hard bump. It went up, high over the net. When my brain figured out it was going to fall straight down towards me, my heart started pounding. But instead of freaking out, like I usually do, I focused.

Time seemed to slow down, and a subtle pink glow crept into the edges of my vision. I fixed my stance, clasping my hands and fingers together properly. I turned my wrists to control where the ball would go after I hit it and then—I waited.

When the ball arrived a second later, I hit it perfectly. It flew back over the net, just where I'd pictured it going. The gym was completely silent. Everyone was so surprised I'd managed to hit the ball, they just watched it until it hit the ground on the other side, scoring a point. My teammates stared at me with their mouths open.

I smiled... but then I saw Jennifer Crawford on the opposing team. I hadn't recognized her at first, with her new haircut. It was chopped short, like a bowl.

Like it so far?

Get the rest for free!

More Free Books

The Scarlet Thread is just one of a dozen novels I'm working on, with completely unique worlds and characters. If you like mermaids, vampires, angels, zombies, revolution, mythology, Faustian motifs (the dangers of technology) and post-apocalyptic or dystopian settings and scenarios, I think you'll enjoy them. Sign up for my free starter library!

>> Sign up at UrbanEpics.com <<

Made in the USA
San Bernardino, CA
14 February 2018